Divine Secrets

Divine Cozy Mystery Series
Book 2

Hope Callaghan

hopecallaghan.com

Visit my website for new releases and special offers:
hopecallaghan.com/newsletter

i

Acknowledgements

Thank you to these wonderful ladies who help make my books shine - Peggy H., Cindi G., Jean P., Wanda D., Barbara W. and Renate P. for taking the time to preview *Divine Secrets,* for the extra sets of eyes and for catching all of my mistakes.

A special THANKS to my reader review team:

Alice, Alta, Amary, Becky, Brinda, Carolyn, Cassie, Charlene, Christina, Debbie, Denota, Devan, Grace, Jan, Jo-Ann, Joyce, Jean K., Jean M., Judith, Katherine, Lynne, Megan, Melda, Kat, Linda, Lynne, Pat, Patsy, Paula, Rebecca, Rita, Tamara, Theresa, Valerie, Vicki and Virginia.

Contents

Chapter 1

"I can't believe you talked me into this." A look of concern crossed Jo's face. "I'm not ready. I need more time to prepare."

Jo's friend, Delta, pressed the palms of her hands over her ears. "I can't hear you," she joked.

Jo playfully slapped her hands away. "You wish you couldn't hear me."

"Tomorrow night will go off without a hitch. The open house will be a huge success, mark my words." Delta patted her boss' back. "Just think...after tomorrow, you and the other lovely ladies who live here will have won the hearts of the Divine townsfolk. They're about to discover that this women's home and the residents who live here are a wonderful addition to the community."

"Or it could reinforce their fears of us and blow up in our faces," Jo said miserably.

"You are such a Negative Nelly. I've been hard at work prepping for our gala event. I know you already approved the dishes, but I still want you to taste test a few I've been tinkering with."

"What is the theme again?" Jo wasn't even sure why Delta decided the open house needed a theme.

"It's not a theme, it's a barbecue. After all, Kansas City is a hop, skip and jump away. You can't have a party in Kansas without barbecue. It's against the law."

"Well, I love barbecue, and if we're trying to make friends, we want to feed them what they want to eat."

"Precisely." Delta hurried to the large pot on top of the stove. "I gotta finish making my famous barbecue sauce."

Jo trailed behind, leaning over Delta's shoulder as she peered into the simmering pot. She wrinkled her nose at the robust aroma. "What's in it?"

"So far, it's minced garlic, minced onion and vanilla."

"Do you need some help?"

"I thought you'd never ask." Delta pulled a tattered recipe card from her apron pocket and handed it to Jo. "This needs to sauté for a couple more minutes before we add the rest of the ingredients."

"Tomato paste, catsup, Worcestershire sauce, apple cider vinegar..." Jo headed to the pantry. "This seems like a lot of work for barbecue sauce."

"Bite your tongue. The store-bought stuff doesn't hold a candle to my sauce."

"Then I can't wait to try it." Jo gathered the remaining ingredients. As soon as Delta gave her the signal, she began dumping them into the large pot while she stirred. "So now what?"

"We let this simmer for a spell before mixing it with the chicken." Delta motioned to a crockpot at the other end of the counter. "The chicken needs shredding."

"Now that's a kitchen chore I can handle." Jo grabbed a couple of dinner forks from the silverware drawer before lifting the lid on the crockpot and pulling the meat apart.

Delta's barbecue sauce finished simmering, and she carried it to the counter. "The pulled pork and turkey are already ready to go. All I need to do is add the secret sauce."

Jo watched her portion out the sauce, distributing it evenly between the three large crockpots. "You cooked an awful lot of meat."

"There's an awful lot of hungry mouths we're gonna have to feed." Delta poured the last of the sauce on top of the shredded chicken.

"Do you think many people will show up?"

Delta waved her wooden spoon at Jo. "Honey, we are going to have the entire town of Divine here tomorrow night."

"I hope not. That's over a thousand people."

"My plan is to have enough food to feed a small army. Now let's give this a stir."

Jo blended the sauce and the chicken while Delta worked her magic on the pulled pork and then the turkey. "Which one would you like to sample?"

"The chicken."

Delta reached for two small plates, handed one to Jo and then reached for a package of slider rolls. "Sherry and Raylene were in here earlier helping me. Raylene's claim that she can't boil water is a bunch of hogwash. That girl has a sense for spices."

"I'm glad you had extra help." Jo scooped a heaping spoonful of meat onto a bun. She carefully set the top on it before taking a small bite. The savory barbecue sauce mixed with a touch of heat gave the slider a slight bite. "The meat has a little zip."

"It's my secret ingredient. Actually, secret ingredients, but I think the main one is the vinegar."

"And the liquid smoke," Jo guessed.

"Yep. I tried making it once without my apple cider vinegar and the taste...it wasn't there."

"You should bottle this sauce up and sell it in the store."

"Now you're talking. We could bottle it up in old mason jars and call it *Delta's Divine BBQ Sauce*."

"That has a rich ring to it." Jo chuckled. "Get it? A ka-ching ring. Tell you what...when you find the time, you should whip up a big batch. We'll do a trial run of selling it in the mercantile. The tourists will eat it up."

Delta rolled her eyes. "You're on a roll today." She laughed as she pointed to the sliders. "Get it? Roll."

"All kidding aside, you should give it some thought." Jo polished off the other half of her slider. "What else do you have?"

"Ribs were too messy, so I decided on some bacon-wrapped smoked sausages." Delta handed Jo a piece of meat, skewered on a toothpick.

Jo inspected the small appetizer. "Is that brown sugar on the outside?"

"Yep. I call this treat a man's candy. No man can resist them. Nash was here earlier and taste-tested a few." Delta shook her head. "Those women sure do like to flirt with poor Nash."

"Nash?" Jo popped the treat in her mouth and tossed the toothpick in the trash.

"Of course. Don't you see how they go gaga over him every time he's around?"

"I hadn't noticed."

Nash Greyson, Jo's handyman, lived in a small apartment above *Second Chance Mercantile*. He'd been with Jo for a few months, and was divorced. His teenage son lived out of state with Nash's ex.

Jo was careful not to pry into Nash's private affairs. He told Jo his son would be visiting for a few weeks during his Christmas break and asked her if it was all right if he stayed with him.

Nash was instrumental in helping Jo run the farm. He'd not only helped her fix up her old Victorian, but he'd also helped renovate the property's mercantile and bakeshop.

He never seemed to get too fired up no matter what crisis was thrown at him. Calm, cool and collected, that's how Jo would describe her right-hand man.

"He's quite a catch."

"What do you mean?"

Delta shoved her hand on her hip. "Joanna Pepperdine, have you ever looked at Nash?"

"Of course. I look at him every day, and I talk to him every day."

"I give up." Delta eased the plate back onto the counter.

"And I better get to work. I want to finish wrapping up my inventory before Pastor Murphy gets here." Jo's mood sobered. Today was the day Raylene Baxter, Jo's newest resident, was leaving.

Pastor Murphy had found a spot for Raylene at a large group home, located between Topeka, Kansas and Kansas City.

"I don't get a good feeling about this new place." Jo contemplated asking Raylene to stay on at the farm, but there was a reason for holding back. The woman's presence was breaking one of Jo's rules...she didn't allow murder convicts.

According to Raylene, her best friend and business partner had been murdered. The woman swore someone else pulled the trigger, although she admitted to being present at the time of the shooting.

She claimed the rigged jury hadn't seen it that way and she had spent the past ten years in prison for her conviction. After her release and with nowhere to go, she'd jumped off *Divine Bridge* and lived.

Evan, a local, had watched Raylene jump. He ran to the edge of the bank to try to help when he noticed two large men dragging her onto the riverbank. By the time Evan reached Raylene, the men were gone.

It was a fall Raylene should not have survived, let alone survived with minor injuries. It was a *Divine Intervention.*

Pastor Murphy visited Raylene in the hospital after the jump and then stopped by Jo's place to ask if she could take her in.

Jo's farm, nicknamed *Second Chance* by the residents, was a halfway house for women recently released from the *Central State Women's Penitentiary.*

After some debate and with Delta dead set against it, Jo allowed Raylene to move in on one condition...the pastor must find a permanent home for her.

The decision had caused some minor issues with the other women, who viewed it as Jo showing favoritism.

Because of Raylene's conviction, an accomplice to murder, the pastor struggled to find a place that would take her. Finally, he had found one.

Delta touched Jo's arm. "You did what you could to help Raylene. God will protect her. He brought her this far."

"You're right. I need to leave it in God's hands." Jo thanked her friend for the pep talk and grabbed her purse. "I guess I better head to the mercantile to finish the inventory."

Fall was right around the corner, and from what Jo had heard the brisk summer business would start to drop off. Visitors to the area would turn into a trickle during the long winter months.

Marlee Davison, Jo's friend and the owner of *Divine Delicatessen*, warned her that after the fall rush it would be quiet until the middle of March, when tourists started returning to the area for the main attraction...a sign and a small church in the middle of nowhere.

The tourist attraction wasn't actually in the middle of *nowhere*. It was the dead center of the forty-eight contiguous United States to be precise. Jo visited the spot once and still had no idea what all of the hoopla was about.

Despite her lack of enthusiasm over the spot, she was thrilled others made the trip. Because *Second Chance Mercantile* and *Divine Baked Goods Shop* were on the main drag leading to the attraction, the shoppers came in droves.

"Send Pastor Murphy out my way when he shows up."

"Will do."

Jo stopped by Raylene's apartment to check to see if she was ready to go. The apartment was empty. Instead, there was a backpack and a small suitcase sitting near the door. She stared at the woman's meager belongings, and sudden tears burned the back of her eyes.

She wanted Raylene to stay. Jo felt God had placed the woman in her care for a reason. She was certain of it, and yet here they were with Raylene leaving. It was breaking Jo's heart.

In fact, she barely slept a wink the night before, having unsettling thoughts about Raylene's future and even dreaming of the woman in trouble and running for her life. Jo mentally shook her head. There was nothing she could do.

She trudged to the mercantile and forced herself to focus on the inventory. She was finishing when

Pastor Murphy, accompanied by a somber Raylene, appeared. "Is it time to go?"

"Yes." Pastor Murphy's expression matched Raylene's expression. "It's a solid three hour drive to Topeka, and I would like to make it back home before dark."

Jo tucked her inventory notes inside the cash register. Sherry, one of the residents and Raylene's closest friend, sniffled. "Are you sure she has to leave?"

"I'm afraid so," Jo said.

Sherry darted around the side of the counter and wrapped her arms around her friend. "I'm going to miss you, Raylene. Please be careful."

"I will." Raylene briefly closed her eyes. "It's going to be okay. I'm going to be okay." She broke free from Sherry's embrace and ran out of the mercantile.

"I wish there was a way she could stay."

"Me, too." Jo squeezed Sherry's arm. "Raylene will be all right. We'll all be praying for her."

The pastor and Jo caught up with Raylene standing next to the pastor's car. "I can't do anymore good-bye's."

"I don't blame you." Jo reached into her purse and pulled out a prepaid cell phone and charger. She handed it to Raylene. "This is for you."

"A cell phone? I...I can't take this." Raylene attempted to hand it back.

"I want you to have it," Jo insisted. "My cell phone number is programmed in the phone. If you ever need me, I'm just a phone call away."

Raylene's eyes watered as she stared at the phone and Jo hurried on. "It has a hundred minutes, and you can put other numbers in the phone, too."

"I don't know anyone else I would want to call, that I could call." Raylene looked as if she was going to burst into tears. She quickly slipped the phone into her pocket and climbed into the back of the car.

Jo opened the passenger door, and a movement caught her eye. The living room curtains fluttered, and she knew Delta was standing behind them, watching them leave.

Delta had said good-bye to Raylene after breakfast and then bolted from the room, something Jo wanted to do, but knew she couldn't. She had to put on a brave face for the woman.

During the long drive, the pastor and Jo attempted to encourage Raylene, but for the most part, she wasn't in the mood to talk. Not that Jo could blame her. Finally, as they drew closer, Raylene asked a question.

"How many women live in the home?"

"Thirty...thirty women. There are twenty-nine now. You'll be the thirtieth." Pastor Murphy had pulled some strings to get Raylene into the house, with promises she was a model resident and offering Jo as a recommendation.

"What about rules?" Jo asked. "I mean, I realize it's not *Second Chance,* but I am curious. I'm sure they have rules in place."

"There are rules." The pastor shot Jo an inquisitive look. "Do you set a curfew?"

"No," Jo shook her head. "There's no need since we're semi-isolated and there's nowhere for the women to go."

"There is a curfew." The pastor glanced in the rearview mirror. "My guess is because the facility is located closer to the city, a curfew is a necessity."

"I have a copy of the rules you gave me this morning." Raylene reached into her backpack and pulled out a folded sheet of paper. "The curfew is six p.m. to seven a.m."

"Six in the evening?" Jo gasped. "That's barely enough time for the women to eat."

"It doesn't matter," Raylene said. "At least I have somewhere to go."

"Let me see the paper." Jo stuck her hand over the seat, and Raylene handed it to her.

She rattled off the list:

"Resident must remain sober. Drug and alcohol use is not allowed, and resident is subject to random drug testing.

Resident must contribute to the house by doing chores.

Fighting or violence toward other residents is grounds for immediate removal.

Stealing or destroying another resident's property is grounds for immediate removal.

Resident must adhere to a curfew. Curfew hours are: 6:00 p.m. until 7:00 a.m.

Resident may be required to attend a 12-step or other recovery meetings.

Resident may be required to interview for jobs if they don't already have one."

Jo handed the paper back. "The rules are similar to mine, except for my random inspections and I don't have a curfew. I guess if I ever have a problem with missing residents, I could amend the rules."

"I think you got it right," Pastor Murphy said. "The right amount of rules and the right amount of freedom."

"Before I forget, I just want to thank you again for taking me in. The women...they love you, Jo," Raylene said quietly. "Why you started a group home for women like us is beyond me. I don't think I could do what you've done. You must have a special reason for opening a halfway house."

Raylene's comment hit home and pierced Jo's heart. She was right...there was a special reason why Jo had purchased *Second Chance* and why she was determined to succeed in helping the women. Someone close to her had desperately needed a second chance but never got it.

"Thank you, Raylene. That means a lot to me. As for you, we must trust God…" Her voice trailed off, and Jo didn't finish her sentence.

There was nothing she could do now. Raylene's immediate future was set.

They hit a small amount of traffic after Topeka and finally pulled off the highway onto a side street. Jo's heart sank as she stared out the window. The farther they went, the seedier the area became. "Are you sure we're heading in the right direction?"

"Yes. We're almost there." The pastor turned onto another side street. A police car, its sirens blaring and lights flashing, flew up behind them. He pulled off to the side to let the car pass.

Pastor Murphy pulled back onto the street and followed the patrol car until they were forced to stop. "What in the world?"

Chapter 2

A cluster of cop cars blocked the street.

"I wonder what's going on." Jo peered anxiously through the windshield.

"I have no idea."

A police officer approached the pastor's vehicle, and he rolled down the window. "We're trying to get to *New Beginnings of Greater Kansas*. It's a halfway house for women."

"You aren't going to get there anytime soon," the officer said.

"Perhaps I could circle around the other side," Pastor Murphy suggested.

"No. There's a hostage situation inside *New Beginnings*. This is as close as you're going to get until the incident is resolved."

Jo unbuckled her seatbelt and leaned across the seat. She glanced at the officer's nametag. "Officer Hayden, do you mean to tell us someone inside has taken a hostage?"

"Hostages," the officer said. "I'm not sure how long it will be before we're able to clear the area. You may want to come back tomorrow."

The pastor shot Jo a helpless look.

"No." Jo firmly shook her head. "We won't be doing that." There was no way she could leave Raylene here. This was exactly what Jo feared. "We are not coming back. Let's go home."

Pastor Murphy thanked the officer and rolled the window up before turning the car around.

Jo waited until they were back on the highway. "Raylene, I do not think *New Beginnings* is the place for you. We're going back to the farm until we figure something else out. Is that all right with you?"

"It's more than all right. Thank you, Jo. I'm sorry to keep causing you so much trouble."

"This isn't your fault, and there's no need to apologize." Jo was certain God did not want Raylene at that halfway house. What were the chances that the day they showed up, the place was involved in a hostage situation? No, God had other plans for Raylene, and it didn't include *New Beginnings*.

The return trip home sped by, and soon Pastor Murphy pulled into Jo's drive. He circled around and stopped near the front steps before shifting into park. "I'm sorry this trip was a waste of time."

"It wasn't a waste of time." Jo unbuckled her seatbelt. "It was a confirmation...a confirmation Raylene is not meant to be in that large group home."

"So you don't want me to try to reach out to them tomorrow, to re-schedule a time for Raylene?"

"I don't." Jo turned to Raylene, still seated in the back. "Do you want to go back there?"

"No. If I had my way…"

"If you had a choice, what would you do?" Jo's tone softened.

"I would stay," Raylene answered in a tight voice. "I would stay right here."

Jo nodded, and opened the passenger door. "Thank you for making the long trip, Sawyer. Raylene and I are both in agreement that *New Beginnings* isn't right for her."

"You know openings in these homes are few and far between," the pastor warned.

Jo followed him to the back of the car where he removed Raylene's suitcase. "Yes, and I appreciate your efforts on our behalf. I know you worked hard to find a spot for Raylene."

"If that's your decision, I'll keep looking. We'll find something eventually." He climbed back into his car as Raylene and Jo stood off to the side.

They waved good-bye and then Jo turned to Raylene. "I'm sorry this didn't work out. I believe God has other plans for you."

"Me, too." Raylene slung her backpack over her shoulder and picked up her suitcase. "I mean, I'm glad it didn't work out, and I believe God has other plans for me."

"Why don't you go on back to your apartment and unpack." Jo pulled the apartment keys Raylene had given her from her purse and handed them to her. "It looks like you may be here for a while."

"I can only hope." Raylene gave Jo a half-hearted smile. "Maybe he'll never find a place for me, and I'll be here for a long time." She handed the cell phone to Jo. "I guess I won't need this now."

"No, I guess you won't." Jo watched Raylene make her way across the driveway and disappear around the side of the buildings before slowly making her way up the porch steps.

She found Delta in the kitchen, hovering over the stove.

"Well? How did it go? Did the halfway house meet your approval? What did Raylene think?"

"You're not going to believe this." Jo poured out the story, of how they arrived to find the street blocked by police cars and the halfway house in the midst of a hostage situation.

Delta pressed a hand to her lips. "Oh, dear heavens. You didn't leave Raylene there, did you?"

"No way. I told Pastor Murphy to turn around and come home. I am not taking Raylene back there. I believe it was God's way of sending a clear message that this is not the place for her. She came back with us and is unpacking now."

"But he barely got her in there," Delta said. "What are you going to do?"

"I don't know. I don't think a large women's home is going to work. You know the statistics as well as I do. Women who move into large group

26

homes in large cities have less than a fifty percent chance of successfully starting over."

Jo sucked in a breath. "The deck is stacked against her. She's been convicted of a serious crime, and she has no family and friends. If she leaves, her chances of staying out of trouble and out of prison are slim to grim."

Delta scratched her chin, eyeing her friend thoughtfully. "You know how I felt about Raylene moving in in the first place."

"You were dead set against it."

"I was. I hate to admit it when I'm wrong, but I think I was wrong about Raylene. I think she is a good fit for *Second Chance*. She's headstrong and stubborn at times, but I see her heart and her intentions, and that she's really trying. I see no problem with her staying, other than your rule."

"There has to be something we can do," Jo said.

"Most of the women like Raylene, but there are one or two. I hear the comments. They still view her presence as you showing some favoritism."

"I'm in a pickle," Jo sighed. "I'll give it some thought. For now, put me to work."

The women got busy, chopping, dicing and prepping for the following day's festivities.

Nash stopped by a short time later to check on them and to go over some final details for the open house. Jo also suspected he was there to find out about Raylene.

"Raylene came back with us," Jo said.

"She did?"

Jo repeated the story, and Nash let out a low whistle. "Now that's another divine intervention. What are you going to do?"

"Pastor Murphy promised to keep looking."

"And we're going to keep praying," Delta said.

"If you don't need me, I think I'll finish cleaning up the workshop before supper. Tomorrow will be a busy day."

Jo touched Nash's arm. "Thank you so much, Nash. I don't know what I would do without you."

Nash looked as if he was about to say something and then changed his mind. Instead, he smiled. "You're welcome, Jo. You know where to find me if you think of anything else that needs to be done."

He strode out of the kitchen and moments later the front porch door slammed.

"Mmm. *Hmm*." Delta jabbed her rolling pin in Jo's direction, pinning her with a stare.

"What?"

"Nash. I've seen it for a while now."

"Seen what?" Jo asked.

"The way he looks at you," Delta replied. "How his voice softens when he speaks to you. How he leans in when you're talking."

"You're crazy," Jo muttered. "Nash is nice to everyone."

"Yep, but he's soft on you, Jo. And you don't even see it."

"Pooh. Nash is too young for me." Jo snatched the rolling pin from Delta's hand. "Stop looking at me like that."

"He's not too young. How old is he?"

"I don't know." Jo waved dismissively. "I can't remember. I think he's somewhere in his mid-forties."

"And you're only in your late forties."

"Too late for love," Jo joked.

Delta lifted a brow.

"Seriously. Don't start playing matchmaker. I have enough on my plate without worrying about the opposite sex."

"I don't know why you're so dead set against falling in love," Delta grabbed a handful of flour and dumped it into her mixing bowl. "You're an attractive woman. He's an attractive *and* interested man."

"Stop." Jo lifted a hand. "Let's talk about something even more unpleasant, like tomorrow's open house."

Finally, Delta gave the subject a rest.

After dinner ended and the kitchen had been cleaned, Jo wandered onto the porch to reflect on the unexpected turn of events. Duke followed behind, flopping down in his usual spot in front of the swing.

Jo kicked off her clogs and rubbed Duke's fur with the bottom of her feet. Her gaze drifted to Nash's workshop on the other side of the driveway. She could see lights on and glanced at her watch.

It was getting late. Maybe Nash had changed his mind. He once told Jo he liked to putter in the evenings, getting things ready for the next morning before his assistant for the day, one of the women, showed up to learn the tools of the trade.

She thought about Delta's absurd suggestion that Nash was showing an interest in her and mentally shook her head. Of course, he was nice to her...she was his boss.

Nash was nice to everyone. Delta was making a mountain out of a molehill.

Jo shifted her gaze to the front of the store. Tomorrow would be hectic, and Jo was the first to admit she was nervous about the open house.

Would anyone show up? If they did, what would they say? How would they react to the women? The last thing Jo wanted was for someone to make a careless comment to one of the residents.

Despite having spent years in a tough environment, they were emotionally fragile, Jo suspected because they spent their years of incarceration doing whatever they had to just to survive.

A yawn escaped Jo's lips, and she covered her mouth. "Okay, Duke. It's time for bed. Tomorrow is going to be one busy day."

Chapter 3

Jo woke early the next morning. It was all hands on deck in the kitchen to help whip up a quick breakfast before Delta kicked everyone out. Michelle, the resident who would be assisting her in the kitchen, stayed behind.

Jo spent the morning darting back and forth between the baked goods shop and the mercantile to make sure everything was in order. After lunch, she decided to stop by the workshop to check on Nash.

She ran into him pushing an old wooden wheelbarrow across the parking lot. Inside the wheelbarrow was a stack of bushel baskets. "What are you doing?"

"Working on my latest brainstorm," Nash set the wheelbarrow down. "I'm putting together a display for your garden produce."

Jo had managed to create the perfect shopping environments for both her baked goods shop and the mercantile, but she still hadn't come up with the perfect setup for selling her garden produce.

She'd tested several different produce displays, but no matter what she tried, they somehow always managed to get lost in the shuffle.

The results had been even worse when she assembled a shelf arrangement inside the bakeshop. She quickly discovered shoppers weren't interested in healthy eating while perusing the decadent baked goods.

Gary's green thumb was producing an abundance of goodies in the gardens, and with harvest season right around the corner, Jo was growing concerned she wouldn't sell much of the produce. Her gardening endeavors would be a waste of time, not to mention the waste of perfectly saleable produce.

"Follow me." Nash pushed the wheelbarrow onto the porch and to the entrance to the mercantile.

Jo held the door and followed him inside, to the spot separating the mercantile from the bakeshop. Storage cubbies on each side connected the two stores.

Nash positioned the wheelbarrow so that it faced out, and began arranging the empty bushel baskets inside. "My plan is to fill each of the baskets with fruits and vegetables. I found another empty wheelbarrow, so we'll be able to place an identical display on the other side."

He pointed to the cubby on the opposite side. "Shoppers can't miss them, especially if we add a catchy sign to the front."

"I love it," Jo beamed. "Maybe we can even offer a daily special like we do in the bakeshop. I think there are a couple of whiteboards around here somewhere."

"So I have your nod of approval?"

"Absolutely. It's brilliant."

"I'll go grab the other wheelbarrow. It will take me a few minutes to get it cleaned up. It's in the barn, covered in a layer of dust." While Nash left to track down the second display, Jo counted out the bushel baskets.

He returned a short time later, placing the identical wheelbarrow and bushel baskets directly across from the other.

Jo ran into the bakeshop to start gathering up the produce, still tucked away in the corner. She made quick work of filling the bushel baskets with juicy, ripe tomatoes, ears of fresh yellow corn and cucumbers. Heads of cabbage, broccoli and cauliflower rounded out the offerings.

While she arranged the displays, Kelli headed to the mercantile's storage area and returned with two identical whiteboards and dry erase markers.

"Thank you, Kelli." Jo stood back to inspect her handiwork. "What do you think?"

"This is the perfect display," Kelli said. "Jo, you're a genius."

"Not me. This was Nash's idea."

"I come up with a decent idea every once in a while." Nash had returned to inspect Jo's handiwork.

"Don't be so modest. This is perfect. I can't wait to see the sales for the next couple of days." Jo finished pricing the produce and then stopped by the mercantile and the bakeshop to tell the women working about the new produce displays.

On her way out, Jo was thrilled when she noticed a couple of shoppers carrying baskets filled with produce. The new displays were going to be a huge success.

Nash had already returned to his workshop. Jo knocked lightly before stepping inside. "I just wanted to thank you again, Nash."

"You're welcome. I hope you sell baskets full of bountiful goods," he quipped.

"It's already starting to catch the shopper's eyes." She told him how she'd noticed at least a couple of the shoppers, their baskets laden with garden goodies on their way to the checkout.

Excited at the prospect of moving more of the produce, Jo made a beeline for the gardens to inspect the crops.

Gary, her gardener, was back on the job after a recent injury. Since returning to work, Jo insisted he have a helper. Looking back, it was something she should have implemented from the beginning.

Delta and she had nearly perfected the resident's work schedules. The schedules rotated daily, with a woman working in the kitchen, helping Delta. A second spent the day in the workshop with Nash. A third worked in the gardens with Gary. The mercantile and bakeshop each required a worker, which left the sixth woman as a "floater," someone who could fill in wherever needed.

They were short one resident, with only five currently living at *Second Chance,* but that was about to change. A new female resident would be arriving soon.

Jo's last stop was an inspection of the women's apartments and common areas. Everything was spic and span.

By the time Jo showered and returned downstairs to check on the last minute preparations, her stomach was churning, and she felt like throwing up.

"You look like you're fixin' to face a firing squad." Delta handed her a stick of peppermint gum. "Chew on this. It will help settle your stomach."

"Thanks." Jo unwrapped the gum. "And thank you for all of the hard work you put into making this happen."

"You're welcome. This is going to be a huge success. Mark my words."

The start of the open house coincided with the closing hours of the mercantile and bakeshop. The first guests started arriving at six o'clock on the dot.

Jo joined her residents, who stood near the entrance to the mercantile ready to greet the guests.

The plan was for the women to take turns escorting groups of guests around the property, to explain how *Second Chance* operated and as Delta suggested, "Lay on the charm."

Jo remained stationed near the entrance to the businesses to greet the arrivals. Finally, the cars stopped rolling in; the parking lot was packed, forcing guests to park their cars along the main road.

The party was in full swing when Jo started making her rounds. She stopped by Nash's workshop first, where she found several locals including Wayne Malton, the owner of *Tool Time Hardware,* inside.

Jo remembered meeting Wayne a couple of weeks earlier when Nash and she had visited the hardware store to purchase surveillance equipment and motion sensor lights.

"Hello, Mr. Malton. Thank you for stopping by."

"Thank you for the invite. You have an amazing setup, Ms. Pepperdine. You put some real thought not to mention elbow grease into making this old place shine," Wayne said. "No wonder Jesse and his sister are bitter."

A petite brunette with sharp green eyes stood by Wayne's side. "I don't believe you've met my wife, Charlotte. Charlotte, this is Joanna Pepperdine, the owner."

"It's so nice to meet you." Charlotte extended her hand and smiled warmly. "Wayne has been saying we needed to get out here to check out what you've done to the place. When we got the invitation, I couldn't wait to finally meet you and find out what all of the fuss was about."

The woman released Jo's hand. "Wayne and I took a tour with one of the residents, Leah. It's just amazing what you've accomplished."

The owner of the hardware store slipped an arm around his wife's waist. "Nash and I were discussing setting up a store account for you. From now on, we're going to give you a ten percent discount at the hardware store. It's our way of contributing to the special work you're doing here."

A flush of warmth ran through Jo at the glowing praise. "I-I thank you."

"Jo is not only a beautiful and strong woman, but she's also our special angel." Nash stepped close to Jo, placing a light hand on her shoulder.

"You are all too kind." Jo, acutely aware of Nash's closeness, could feel her cheeks redden as her pulse ticked up a notch. "It is so nice to meet you, Charlotte."

Nash stepped away as the four of them made small talk. All Jo could think about was Nash's hand, and she had trouble keeping up with the conversation.

"I-I need to go check on Delta." Jo quickly excused herself, rushing out of the workshop. She stepped onto the stoop and pressed a hand to her beating heart.

"This is your fault, Delta," Jo muttered under her breath. "It's your fault for putting crazy thoughts in my head."

She forced herself to take several deep breaths; all the while scolding herself for thinking Nash might be interested. The last thing Jo needed was a man in her life.

She'd already tried marriage once, many years ago. The marriage lasted a few short years before Gabe and she split amicably. The couple had never started a family.

Jo's parents were dead, and their deaths were something she refused to dwell on. It brought up too many painful memories. Jo forced the thought of her parents out of her mind. God had put her exactly where she needed to be.

The women, along with Delta, Nash and Gary were her family, and Jo Pepperdine was here to stay.

Everyone she'd met so far seemed genuinely interested in *Second Chance* and complimented Jo on embarking on such a selfless endeavor. She was beginning to think that perhaps Delta was right. Not all of the local residents were against her, and the open house hadn't been such a bad idea after all.

There were a couple, including the relatives of the previous owners, who held a grudge against Jo. Perhaps one day they, too, would change their minds.

Even without the McDougall's blessing, it appeared Jo and the women were being welcomed into Divine, into the small town community, and for that, Jo was deeply grateful.

She slowly crossed the drive, making her way to the stately Victorian house, ablaze with lights, beckoning friends and new acquaintances inside.

As Jo drew closer, she could hear the sound of voices drifting onto the porch. She stepped into the living room, smiling as she passed by several guests and made her way into the dining room.

Delta had created a lavish spread. Along with the barbecue sliders, there were also maple bacon smokies, bowls of homemade coleslaw and potato salad, a vegetable platter, baked beans, and sweet dinner rolls.

For dessert, Delta had whipped up an assortment of tasty treats. There were three kinds of cookies, along with cheesecake bites; some drizzled with chocolate, others with strawberry. Among them was Jo's favorite, cheesecake topped with chocolate chips and walnuts.

There was an array of refreshments...sweet tea, lemonade, Delta's special blend of fruit punch and of course, the usual coffee and tea at a side table.

Jo inspected the kitchen and began bagging up the overflowing trash. She was on her way to the bin near the back steps when Sherry bolted into the kitchen, nearly colliding with Jo. "There you are. Delta is looking for you."

Chapter 4

Jo followed Sherry into the dining room where Delta stood near the beverage table talking to a plump woman, with curly blond hair, someone Jo hadn't met yet. "Sherry said you needed me. What's going on?"

"I found this in your downstairs bathroom, on the windowsill." The woman handed Jo a wallet. "I didn't look inside."

"One of the guests left their wallet in the bathroom?" Jo turned it over in her hand. She flipped the wallet open, and her eyes squinted as she studied the license in the holder. "Craig Grasmeyer."

"Craig...Grasmeyer?" The woman's eyes grew wide.

"You know who this is Ms..." Jo's voice trailed off.

"Carrie. I'm Carrie Ford," the woman replied. "We haven't met yet."

"Carrie lives just outside of town," Delta said. "Her husband."

"Deceased husband," Carrie corrected. "I'm a widow."

Jo extended a hand. "It's my pleasure to meet you, Mrs. Ford. This wallet belongs to a local resident."

"I know who he is, but I haven't seen him. Maybe he just got here and is touring the grounds," Delta said.

"We could split up and try to track him down," Sherry suggested.

"That's an excellent idea." Jo turned the wallet so that Sherry was able to get a good look at the man's photo. "He has to be around here somewhere." She flipped the wallet shut. "I'll start my search in the mercantile and bakeshop. Sherry, you run around to the women's apartments and common area."

"I'll check the parking lot," Delta said. "I don't think anyone has left yet."

"And I'll have a look around inside," Carrie offered. "Grasmeyer drives a black jeep."

"Perfect."

The women split up and began searching for the guest with Jo starting her search inside the mercantile before moving on to the bakeshop.

Kelli was inside the store, waiting to greet the last of the stragglers.

"Hi, Kelli. It looks like everyone has gone over to the house."

"Yeah. I haven't seen anyone for about half an hour."

"I'll lock up, and you can head next door to grab a bite to eat. One of our guests left his wallet on the windowsill in the downstairs bathroom." Jo gave her a glimpse of the man's picture ID. "Do you recall seeing him?"

"Nope." Kelli shook her head. "He doesn't look familiar."

"I hope he hasn't left already." Jo glanced at her watch. "You can take off, and I'll lock up."

"I'm in no hurry. We can go together." Kelli waited for Jo to check the backdoors and turn off the store lights.

She finished locking the front doors, and Sherry joined them on the porch. "Any sign of Mr. Grasmeyer?"

"Nope." Sherry shook her head. "There's no one back there. I think all of the guests have gone inside the house."

The trio crossed the driveway, heading up the front steps and into the living room.

"I think I'll have a quick look upstairs." Jo climbed the stairs, starting the search in her bedroom before making her way down the hall and peeking inside each of the second floor bedrooms. She finished her search at the end of the hall, where she eyed the spiral staircase leading to the widow's walk.

Jo climbed to the top. She slid the bolt and unlocked the door before stepping out into the evening air. The floor creaked loudly as she made her way to the edge of the rotunda.

"Any luck?"

Jo clutched her chest and spun around. "Delta, you scared me half to death."

"Sorry. I thought you heard me."

"How did you find me?"

"Duke. He's sitting at the bottom of the stairs, staring up here like he lost his best friend."

Jo laughed. "Duke doesn't like it because he can't get up the spiral stairs. He's been pouting all night about me not letting him join the party."

"With all of the cars and people coming and going, he's safer hanging out upstairs," Delta said. "I haven't had any luck tracking down Grasmeyer."

"Me, either. Maybe he left."

Delta joined Jo at the railing, keeping one eye on the domed ceiling. "You see any bats in your haunted hangout?"

"This isn't haunted. You should come up here during the day. On a clear day, the views are spectacular."

"I'll take your word for it."

Jo patted the man's wallet in her front pocket. "If Mr. Grasmeyer already left, I'm sure he'll come back when he realizes he lost his wallet."

"If he remembers where he left it," Delta pointed out.

"We could drive to his home and return it." A group of guests caught Jo's attention as they wandered out of the house and onto the driveway. "People are starting to leave. We better get downstairs." Jo followed Delta down the spiral steps.

Duke was waiting for them at the bottom. "It won't be long, and you'll be able to come back downstairs," Jo patted his head. "Maybe the woman…"

"Carrie," Delta said.

"Carrie found Grasmeyer."

"She's a character." Delta reached for the stair rail.

"Character?"

"A busybody or more like a nosy-body. If Grasmeyer is here, she found him."

Carrie wasn't waiting at the bottom of the stairs, but a woman who looked vaguely familiar was. It took a few seconds for Jo to figure out the woman was Debbie Holcomb.

"Debbie Holcomb. I'm surprised to see you."

"Why would you be surprised?" the woman snapped. "I thought everyone in town was invited."

"They were," Jo replied evenly. "I figured since you told me my home was cursed, this would be the last place you would want to be."

"Curiosity got the better of me," Debbie sniffed. "Besides, I've never met a convict before."

Jo could feel her blood beginning to boil. "That was uncalled for. I think it's time for you to leave."

A hushed murmur filled the room, and someone coughed.

"I think Ms. Pepperdine is right." Sheriff Franklin joined the trio.

Holcomb ignored him. "It's such a shame you turned this beautiful home into an eyesore."

Jo clenched her fists, forcing herself to remain calm. "When I purchased this place, it was in a sad state of affairs, almost beyond repair. I spent a good chunk of money, not to mention time, returning this home to its original beauty."

"Beauty?" Holcomb scoffed. "This is nothing but a cheap, cheesy dump now. I wouldn't live here if someone paid me."

"No one is asking you to," Jo gritted out. "You can leave now, or I'll have Sheriff Franklin arrest you for trespassing."

Holcomb's eyes grew wide. "You wouldn't dare!"

"Don't tempt me."

The sheriff stepped between the women. "It's time for you to go, Debbie." He placed a light hand on her arm, and she jerked away.

"I was on my way out anyway. I think the food was either tainted or spoiled. I'm starting to feel sick to my stomach."

Delta's eyes flashed. She made a move toward the woman and Holcomb, noting the thunderous look, quickly hustled toward the front door. "I'll show myself out."

The door slammed behind her, and someone in the crowd choked out a laugh.

Jo could feel a burning from the top of her head to the tips of her toes. There was a light tap on her shoulder. It was Carrie.

"I completely disagree, Ms. Pepperdine. You have a lovely home."

"Thank you, Carrie. Mrs. Ford," Jo said kindly. "Were you able to track down Mr. Grasmeyer?"

"No," Carrie shook her head. "I looked everywhere."

"Is there a problem?" the sheriff asked.

Jo pulled Grasmeyer's wallet from her pocket. "Mrs. Ford found this wallet in our guest bathroom. It appears a local, Craig Grasmeyer, left it behind. We were trying to locate him to return it. Perhaps it would be best if I turned it over to you."

"Of course." The sheriff took the wallet. "Grasmeyer is well-known around town."

Marlee, the owner of the local deli, made her way over. "You did a great job of putting this event together. The tour was my favorite part. I had no idea how much work was involved in keeping this place running."

"I have a lot of help," Jo motioned to Delta. "And Delta is a big part of it."

Carrie swayed slightly before grabbing onto the back of a nearby chair. "Whew. I'm feeling a little lightheaded. Must be all of the excitement."

"You look a little pale." Jo turned to Sherry. "Could you please bring Mrs. Ford a glass of water?"

"Of course." Sherry hurried off, returning moments later. She handed the water to Carrie.

"Thank you. I'm fine, really. I'm probably just tired, and it's time to go home."

Nash appeared at Carrie's side. "I'll walk you to your car."

The sheriff, along with Marlee, Delta and Jo, waited for Nash to escort the woman out of the house.

"She probably wore herself out, snooping around every square inch of the property," Delta said.

"Snooping?" Jo asked.

"Snoopy times a hundred," Marlee sighed. "I caught her in my kitchen last week, rifling through the cabinets. She said she was looking for packets of artificial sweetener."

"Don't you keep sweeteners and sugar on the table?" Jo asked.

"Yep. I think she's bored," Marlee said. "Ever since her most recent husband, Abner, passed away she has too much time on her hands."

"Poor thing," Jo murmured.

The party resumed with Jo making her rounds, meeting several more of the Divine residents. With each conversation, she began to realize Delta knew what she was doing when she insisted on hosting an open house.

The sheriff made his way over. "I'm gonna head out, Ms. Pepperdine. Thank you for opening your home to us. It was high time some of the residents got to know you." He lowered his voice. "You got a nice group of ladies living here, too. Very polite and courteous."

"Thank you. They're wonderful women; in need of a fair shake and a second chance."

"And I think they found the perfect place to get just that."

The sheriff's radio began to squawk. "Sheriff Franklin, do you copy?"

"Never a dull moment." The sheriff lifted his radio. "Go ahead. I'm here."

"We got a report of an automobile accident over on the curves on Silvernail Road. One of the locals called it in."

"A fender bender?" the sheriff asked.

"No. The vehicle ran off the road. It's a red Dodge minivan."

A flicker flashed across the sheriff's face. "It sounds like Carrie Ford's van."

"An ambulance is on the way to the scene."

Chapter 5

The sheriff tipped his hat and dashed out of the house.

Jo followed him as far as the porch and watched as he climbed into his patrol car and sped out of the driveway.

Delta and Marlee joined Jo.

"I hope they're mistaken and Carrie wasn't the one involved in the accident." Jo glanced over her shoulder. "Nash was the last one to see her when he walked her out. Perhaps we shouldn't have let her leave after she said she was feeling lightheaded."

"You can't hold yourself responsible," Marlee said. "Those curves over on Silvernail Road are treacherous, even during the day."

Leah, one of the residents, appeared in the doorway. "Is everything okay?"

"It appears one of our guests may have been involved in some sort of an automobile accident on her way home," Jo said.

"Excuse me. I'm just gonna sneak by you, dear." A woman joined Leah in the doorway, purse in hand.

"You're leaving?" Leah held the door for the woman.

"Yes, I need to get going. My poor pup, Curlie, is home waiting for me. Thank you for hosting such a wonderful event."

"You're welcome." Jo thanked the woman for stopping by, and more guests followed behind until almost everyone had departed.

Claire, the owner of *Claire's Collectibles* and Divine's only coin laundromat, was the last to leave. "I'm sorry to hear about Carrie's accident."

"News sure does spread fast," Jo said. "We don't know for sure that it was Carrie."

"It was," Claire nodded. "I spoke with Jen, one of the laundromat's part-time employees. Her cousin, Evelyn, works for the sheriff's department. She told her it was Carrie who was involved in the crash."

"I need to talk to Nash. Surely, he would not have allowed the woman to get behind the wheel if he thought she was unfit to drive."

"While you do that, I'll round up the gals to help me clean up the mess," Delta said.

"I'll be back shortly to help." Jo walked Claire to her car and then stopped by Nash's workshop.

The lights were off and the door locked. She lifted her eyes to his second story apartment above the mercantile. A dim light flickered in the living room window.

Jo slowly climbed the steps. When she reached the top, she gave the door a couple of quick raps.

There was a muffled rattling noise coming from inside the apartment, and then the door opened.

"Jo." Nash appeared in the doorway, his hair damp and holding a towel.

Flustered, Jo quickly averted her gaze. "I'm sorry to bother you, Nash. I...I wondered if you had a minute to talk."

"Of course." Nash motioned Jo into his apartment. "I just finished cleaning up. Let me take care of my towel."

She hesitated for a second before stepping inside. Nash closed the door behind them. "I'll be right back."

He returned moments later. "Sorry about that. I typically don't get evening visitors."

"No need to apologize. I didn't mean to show up unannounced. It's about Carrie Ford, the woman you escorted to her van earlier this evening."

Nash chuckled. "Carrie's a trip. She was fishing for an invitation back to my apartment. Is everything all right?"

"The sheriff got a call about an accident over on Silvernail Road, not long after Carrie left. Rumor has it that she may have been involved."

"No kidding," Nash shook his head. "She seemed okay when she left, but the curves on that road are treacherous even in the daytime."

"That's why I'm here, to ask if you thought she seemed okay to drive home. She was complaining about feeling lightheaded before she left."

"I never would've let her leave if I was concerned, but now that you mention it she sat in her van for a long time before driving off. I almost went back over to check on her."

"So maybe she was stricken by some sort of medical episode," Jo theorized.

"It could be," Nash agreed.

"Again, I'm sorry to bother you this late." Jo stood. "Thank you for walking Carrie to her van and for everything else you do to keep this placing running."

Nash sprang to his feet. "Would you like a cup of coffee or a soda?"

"It's getting late. I need to get back to the house to help Delta and the women finish cleaning up." Jo continued talking as she backed toward the door. "I'll see you in the morning."

"Of course." Nash reached around Jo, opening the door to let her out. "See you in the morning."

"Yes." Jo tripped on the threshold and stumbled onto the landing. "I better watch where I'm going."

"We don't need you tumbling down the stairs," Nash said. "Maybe I should give you a hand," he teased.

"That won't be necessary." Jo gave him a small smile and bolted down the steps. She could feel

Nash's eyes on her until she reached the bottom of the stairs and his apartment door closed.

Irritated by her unexpected reaction, Jo began berating herself and then Delta. *This is ridiculous. You're acting like a love-struck teenager.*

Jo forced Nash from her mind as she tromped across the driveway and back inside the house where Delta and the women were drying the remaining dishes.

Jo grabbed a clean dishtowel from the drawer. "Nash said Carrie seemed fine to drive, but he also said she sat in her van for a long time before leaving. He was getting ready to go check on her and then she took off."

"So maybe something happened to her," Delta said.

"Could be. I'm sure we'll know more tomorrow."

The conversation drifted to the party and everyone agreed it was a huge success. The women claimed they enjoyed the get-together and Jo told them she might consider turning it into an annual event.

Finally, the last dish was dried and put away. Jo thanked everyone for their help; she waited for Delta and the women to head to their apartments before locking up and heading upstairs to her room.

She made quick work of brushing her teeth and putting her pajamas on. Duke waited for Jo to climb into bed before claiming his spot at the end of it.

As Jo drifted off to sleep, she thanked God for a successful open house, and a chance to get to know the area residents. She thanked Him for the women who lived at the farm. Her last prayer was for Carrie Ford, that she wasn't injured.

*****

Jo woke early the next morning, her to-do list first and foremost in her mind. Saturday was grocery day.

Delta typically accompanied Jo to the local superstore in Centerpoint Junction, one of the nearby larger towns, but she'd told Jo she promised to help her niece, Patti, finish tearing down some old wallpaper in what was once Delta's bedroom.

Instead, Michelle, one of the residents, offered to accompany Jo. Michelle was one of the quieter residents. Even though she pitched in and handled all of the jobs assigned to her, she kept to herself during her off hours.

Michelle was a stark contrast to the others, who were much more vocal. The quiet concerned Jo slightly, and she saw the one-on-one shopping trip as the perfect opportunity to get to know her.

Saturday breakfasts were a fend-for-yourself event since Delta was off on Saturday mornings, but there was plenty of cold cereal and fruit available. Jo poured a bowl of frosted flakes and was standing in the kitchen eating it when Michelle wandered in.

"Are you ready for our big shopping day?"

Michelle wrinkled her nose. "I'm not big on shopping. I do want to pick up a few odds and ends." She pulled a folded sheet of paper from her pants pocket. "I offered to pick up some things for the others, too. I hope you don't mind."

Jo set the cereal bowl on the counter. "Not at all. In fact, I think the gesture is very thoughtful of you."

"Thanks. We can pick this stuff up at *Divine Pharmacy*, but it's a lot cheaper at the bigger store."

"I'm almost ready." Jo finished her cereal and rinsed the bowl before placing it inside the dishwasher. "If we leave now, we can get an early start and be back before it gets too late."

Delta was already long gone, so Jo made sure the kitchen was tidy before she grabbed her SUV keys, and Michelle and she headed to the garage out back.

She unlocked the doors and started to climb inside when she spotted a patrol car pulling into the driveway. It was Deputy Brian Franklin, Sheriff Bill Franklin's son. He exited the car and made his way over.

"Hey, Jo." The deputy tipped his hat to Michelle. "Ma'am."

"Hello, Deputy Franklin. To what do I owe the pleasure of an early morning visit?"

"One of the local residents, Carrie Ford, was involved in an automobile accident last night."

"I heard." Jo leaned against the side of the SUV. "Your father got the call while he was here. I hope she's going to be all right."

"She's a little banged up. Lucky for her she was wearing her seatbelt."

"I'm glad to hear that," Jo said. "Thank you for letting me know."

"This isn't a social call." The young deputy shifted his feet. "There's something else."

Jo's stomach knotted at the tone of the deputy's voice. "Then why are you here?"

"Ms. Ford said someone followed her from the open house and forced her van off the road."

Chapter 6

"Ran her off the road?" Jo gasped.

"That's what she claims. In fact, she thinks it may have been a larger vehicle, a pickup truck similar to the one you own."

"Nash mostly drives the truck. He would never do such a thing. He escorted her to her van and then watched her drive off."

The deputy looked increasingly uncomfortable. "I would like to ask Mr. Greyson a few questions if you don't mind."

"Of course not." Jo tossed the SUV keys to Michelle and then escorted the deputy across the driveway to Nash's workshop.

As she got close, she could hear the loud buzz of the table saw. Jo didn't bother knocking. Instead, she pushed the door open and stepped inside. "Hey, Nash."

"Nash!"

He shut the saw off and removed his earplugs. "Hey, Jo. I thought you left already."

"Not yet. Deputy Franklin is here. He would like to ask you a few questions about Carrie."

Nash glanced over his shoulder. "Hello."

"Hey, Nash." The deputy cleared his throat. "I'll only take a moment of your time." He briefly repeated what he'd told Jo, how Carrie swore someone followed her from the farm and forced her van off the road.

"You're kidding." Nash dropped his earplugs on the workbench. "I watched Carrie leave. I don't recall anyone following her out."

"I wish I was." The deputy removed a notepad and pen from his front pocket. "I'm sure there are plenty of witnesses who can verify you were here at the time of the accident."

"No."

"No, you don't have witnesses?" The man paused, pen in hand.

"Unfortunately, after I watched Mrs. Ford leave, I came here to my workshop to clean up and then I went upstairs to my apartment. I'm not big on parties."

"So no one can verify you were still here at the time of Carrie's accident?" The deputy began scribbling furiously.

"This is absurd," Jo interrupted. "Nash has no reason to harm Carrie."

"Are you certain that there isn't someone, perhaps one of the residents, who may be able to corroborate your claim of being here at the time of the accident?"

"It's not a claim," Nash said quietly. "It's the truth and no. The only other person I saw after Carrie was Jo. She stopped by my apartment last night before turning in."

"Nash." Jo touched his arm. "We should double check with the women. Maybe one of them left the party to head back to their apartment and saw you, even though you didn't see them."

"That's an excellent idea," Deputy Franklin said.

Jo walked to the door. "I'll go round up the residents."

"Wait." The deputy lifted a hand. "I hate to be the bearer of all of this bad news, but there's something else."

Before the deputy could finish, there was a light knock on the door, and Sheriff Franklin appeared in the doorway. He wasn't alone. Two solemn-faced gentlemen stood directly behind him.

"Joanna Pepperdine."

"Yes."

"I have a warrant to search your premises."

"Search my property? Why?"

"Craig Grasmeyer's employee just filed a missing person's report on him."

"But...he must have been here for the open house," Jo shook her head, confused. "Carrie Ford found his wallet in our guest bathroom."

"I was here for part of the open house. I don't recall seeing Grasmeyer. Are you saying you saw him?"

"No...no." Jo pressed a hand to her forehead, her mind whirling. "Carrie, Delta, Sherry, and I...we all searched the place but were unable to locate him. We figured he'd already left. That's why I gave you his wallet."

"I visited his private residence first thing this morning to return it to him. He wasn't home, so I stopped by his lumberyard. His employee, Ms.

Talbot, told me she hasn't been able to reach him for a couple of days."

"So now you think I have something to do with his disappearance? I've never even met the man."

"Then letting us search your property is only a formality."

"I have nothing to hide." Jo led the sheriff out of the workshop and back to the house, stopping when she reached the porch. She waited for the other two men to catch up. "You're not going to find anything."

Sheriff Franklin motioned to one of the men. "You start searching the outbuildings. Jim, you start upstairs. I'll start here."

The young Deputy Franklin joined them as his father barked the orders. "I'm heading out." He turned to Jo. "Sorry to have to spring this on you, Ms. Pepperdine."

"There's no need to apologize. I hope you find the missing man, but I can assure you that you won't find him here."

It wasn't the deputy or even the sheriff's fault they were searching her place. And maybe it wasn't even Carrie's fault. Obviously, something happened to her on her way home, whether it was a medical episode or something more sinister.

The deputy left and Sheriff Franklin passed Jo on his way inside.

She started to follow behind and then changed her mind. Instead, Jo eased onto the porch swing, her eyes wandering to the farm field across the street. Surely, the authorities couldn't possibly believe she would place the man's wallet in her bathroom for a guest to find...and a missing man at that.

Restless, Jo slid off the swing and wandered inside where she found the sheriff in her office, leaning over her desk.

"I'm not hiding a missing man on top of my desk." Jo leaned her hip against the door and studied the sheriff.

"I was admiring how tidy your desk is. Mine is a junk pile."

"I have to stay organized. Otherwise..." Jo made a downward motion with her thumb. "Running this place is more than a full-time job."

The sheriff nodded and slowly turned, studying the woman in the doorway. "I owe you an apology."

"Apology?"

"Yes. Strangers don't come 'round these parts and move into town, let alone purchase the biggest piece of property on the block. You caused quite a stir."

Jo chuckled. "Especially with Debbie Holcomb and her brother, the postmaster."

"Yep. I wouldn't worry much about them. They weren't gonna be happy with the new owners, no matter who it was."

"I'm sure it didn't help once folks found out about the women moving in."

"Nope." The sheriff shoved his hands in his pockets. "We got enough goings on with the busybodies around here, including Carrie. This place gives 'em one more reason to yap at the jaws."

"I'm sure it does."

"Back to my apology...I was one of the first to think a halfway house for former convicts was gonna be nothing but trouble." He rocked back on his heels. "Last night's open house changed my mind. I admire you, Joanna Pepperdine. Most people, they talk about doing the right thing. You're actually making a difference, for all of these women."

Jo felt her throat swell and she swallowed hard. She never was good at accepting a compliment. "I...thanks."

"So don't let those old naysayers get you down."

"I'll keep that in mind." Jo changed the subject. "So I guess you don't think I have a body hidden somewhere around here."

"Not if you have half a brain, which I think you do. Could be Grasmeyer left town. He and his wife are in the midst of a nasty divorce. We've already contacted her to see if she has any idea where her husband might be."

"But why would his wallet, with credit cards and identification inside, be in my bathroom?" Jo asked.

"I haven't the slightest, which is why I'm here - to follow up and try to trace his steps. With any luck, he'll show up."

"Someone mentioned he wasn't well-liked around town."

"You could say that," the sheriff replied. "But being unpopular and in his case, unpleasant isn't a crime."

Jo moved to the side to let the sheriff pass by. "I'll have a look around the living room and then maybe check the cellar."

"I don't go down there often. It's dank, dark and creepy."

"I'm sure you've heard the rumors about this place."

"Debbie Holcomb told me the farm is cursed, but I figured she was just trying to scare me."

Franklin adjusted his hat. "This property abuts up against the Indian reservation to the south."

"I think I remember Nash mentioning it." Jo had heard about the Indian reservation, not far from Divine. According to Delta, the reservation was home to *Kansas Creek Tribe*. The Native Americans also operated a small retail shopping area on the reservation.

"Local lore claims this property was once owned by the tribe and used as a burial site. There was an uprising not long after the government deeded the land to the tribe. Two of the tribal leaders and their men fought for power."

"Here?" Jo asked.

"Yes. One of the leaders and several of his warriors were slaughtered. They called this the *Field of Blood*. The Indians refused to settle the *Field of Blood* and returned the property to the government, who in turn sold it to the McDougalls."

"That's why Debbie Holcomb said it was cursed."

"If you believe it." The sheriff exited Jo's office and made his way into the living room. He picked up the fireplace poker and poked at the cold ashes before returning it to the stand. "I'll have a quick look in the cellar."

"You can use the set of stairs off the kitchen. There's also an outside entrance, a set of double doors around the side of the house. Like I said, I rarely go down there. Delta plans to clean it up and use it to store canned goods this winter."

The sheriff followed Jo through the kitchen and into the mudroom near the back door. She pointed to a scuffed door with peeling paint. "This is it."

The cellar project was on Jo's to-do list, but with so many other repairs needing urgent attention, it was at the bottom of the list.

Jo flipped the switch, and the single bare bulb pierced the darkness, giving off a dull yellow glow. The damp smell of mildew drifted up. "It's not a pretty place," Jo warned.

"Neither is mine," the sheriff said. "During tornado season, I wouldn't trade my smelly old cellar for a bag of gold."

"True. Is tornado season as scary as everyone around here says?"

"Yes, ma'am. It can be downright deadly. We're smack dab in tornado alley. If you hear those sirens and get that warning, you best head straight to the cellar. Tornadoes are nothing to mess with."

"Thank you for the warning." Jo reached the bottom of the stairs and stepped off to the side. "There's another light in the center of the room. See the string hanging down?"

"Yep." The sheriff crossed to the center of the dank space and tugged on the string. More dull yellow light illuminated the space. His eyes slowly scanned the room before he made his way to the second set of steps.

"Are these the exterior cellar doors you were talking about?"

"They are." Jo nodded. "They open to the other side of the house, to the right of the kitchen."

He ascended the narrow cement steps, the crumbling concrete crunching under his steel-toed boots.

"It's locked." Jo tiptoed to the bottom step.

The sheriff climbed to the top, placing the palms of his hands on each side. The doors creaked open, and bright sunlight poured in.

"These doors should be locked." Jo hurried up the steps and followed him onto the lawn.

Franklin dropped the doors back in place and inspected the exterior. "The lock is gone."

Sure enough, the padlock was missing. "That's odd. Maybe Nash was down here looking for something."

"I'll need to take a closer look." The sheriff flung the doors open and traipsed down the steps. He abruptly stopped when he reached the bottom step. "I think I found something."

Chapter 7

Jo hurried down the steps. "What is it?"

"It looks like blood." The sheriff plucked his radio from his belt. "Art, do you copy?"

"Go ahead, Bill."

"I got something in the main house, on the cellar steps. I'll need a bottle and swab for a sample."

"I'm on my way."

Jo stared at the red splotch in disbelief. "The door should have been locked."

"When's the last time you checked the lock?" the sheriff asked.

"Gosh. I don't know." Jo started to pace. "It's been at least a couple of weeks. Like I said, we keep it padlocked."

Raylene appeared at the top of the stairs. "Is everything all right?"

"No. The cellar was unlocked, and it looks like there's fresh blood on the steps."

"Seriously?" Raylene cautiously made her way down the steps and joined Jo, who pointed at the splotch.

"The splotch isn't fresh." Raylene leaned in for a closer look. "See how the edges are dry?"

Raylene carefully sidestepped the spot, easing past the sheriff before she slowly climbed the stairs and stepped onto the grass. She lifted one of the cellar doors and studied the latch. "There doesn't appear to be any signs of forced entry."

She set the door down and inspected the other door. "My guess is someone either had a key or picked the lock."

The sheriff eyed her curiously. "What are you, some sort of crime scene investigator?"

Raylene cast Jo an uneasy glance. "I should keep my opinions to myself."

"No." Jo shook her head. "I need all of the help I can get. So you think the splotch of blood has been there for some time and that there was no forced entry?"

"Correct," Raylene confirmed. "Again, it's just my personal observation."

The investigator, Art, joined them near the top of the stairs and Sheriff Franklin motioned him down. "We might have something here."

While the investigator swabbed the mysterious spot, Jo pulled Raylene off to the side. "I think someone is trying to frame us. Last night at the open house, one of our guests found a man's wallet in the downstairs bathroom. It turns out the man, Craig Grasmeyer, is missing. The same guest claims a vehicle similar to our pickup truck followed her and forced her off the road last night. Now, this."

"The man could be anywhere," Raylene said. "Could be he was here at the party, and you didn't see him."

"I'm hoping he left and we somehow missed him. You just gave me an idea. I'm going to have Nash check the surveillance cameras."

"Do you have your cell phone with you?" Raylene asked.

"Yeah." Jo pulled it from her pocket and handed it to her.

"We need to take some pictures, just in case." Raylene snapped several pictures of the cellar doors. She eased onto the steps and snapped a picture of the sheriff and the investigator, still examining the splotch.

After she finished, she handed the phone to Jo and then pressed a finger to her lips as she motioned to the men who were talking in hushed voices.

"...broadcast..."

Raylene took a tentative step toward the men. "Maybe it was Gary, our gardener, who was down here. He could have accidentally cut himself, or even Nash."

The sheriff's eyes squinted. "You sure do have a lot of theories, Ms..."

"Raylene. Raylene Baxter."

"Huh." The sheriff tilted his head. "How do you know so much?"

"I have a little background in investigations," Raylene glanced at Jo, who nodded. "Go ahead. You can tell him."

"I was a bond agent in Florida, or what you call a bounty hunter. I spent my fair share of time tracking people down and searching for clues."

"What an intriguing line of work for such a young woman."

"I'm not that young."

The investigator finished collecting the sample, and the men spent several minutes scouring the cellar before joining the women on the lawn. "According to Art, none of the women or residents are able to corroborate Nash Greyson's claim he never left the property last night."

"I stopped by his apartment after the open house ended." Jo crossed her arms. "You know as well as I do that Nash did not follow Carrie and then run her off the road. If I were you, I would take a closer look at Grasmeyer's employee."

"Rest assured we'll be investigating every angle," the sheriff said.

The men returned to their vehicles, where the third investigator stood near the back of the van, studying an open laptop.

Jo grabbed Raylene's hand, and they followed behind.

"What do you say, Jim?" Franklin asked.

"I just got a call back from headquarters. They finished going over Mrs. Ford's vehicle for signs of exterior damage. There's some damage near the rear quarter panel."

"It's possible she lost control of her vehicle," Jo theorized. "She claimed she was feeling lightheaded right before she left the open house, which is why Nash walked her to her car."

"As I said before, we're still investigating." The sheriff nodded to the man. "I'll see you two back at the station."

"Will do." The investigator closed the lid on the laptop before he and the other man climbed into the unmarked van and backed out of the driveway.

Sheriff Franklin turned his attention to Jo and Raylene. "I apologize for having to spring the search on you."

"I truly hope this is the end of the matter." Jo lifted a finger. "Can you hang tight? I want to ask Gary if he was down in the cellar the other day."

"Of course."

Jo pulled her cell phone from her pocket and dialed Gary's cell phone number. "Hello, Jo."

"Hi, Gary. I'm calling to find out if you were in the cellar recently. The lock is off, and there's a spot of blood on one of the steps."

"The lock is off?"

"Yes, it's missing from the exterior double doors."

"That's my fault. I was down there yesterday before I left. Delta's been pestering me about taking a look at the old canning jars to see if they can be salvaged. I didn't realize one of the jars was broken, and I cut my finger. It started bleeding so I ran back upstairs and must've forgotten to replace the lock."

"That's wonderful, I mean it's awful you cut your finger." Jo shifted the phone to her other ear. "But your accident clears up a lot. How is your finger?"

"Doctor Delta fixed me right up, and it's already on the mend."

"Thanks, Gary. Thank you for letting me know."
Jo disconnected the call and waved the phone in the
air. "Gary was down in the cellar, checking the old
canning jars. He cut his finger on a broken piece of
glass and went upstairs to look for a bandage. He
forgot to replace the lock."

"You're sure?"

"You heard the conversation," Jo scowled. "If you
don't believe me, you can ask Gary yourself."

"Whoa." The sheriff lifted both hands. "No reason
to get testy."

"I'm sorry. I didn't mean to snap. I'm a little
freaked out about the missing man and wondering
why his wallet was here."

"Hopefully, we'll have some news on Grasmeyer
soon."

After the sheriff departed, Jo tracked Michelle
down for the trip to town. During the ride, Jo asked
Michelle about life on the farm. The woman's
answers were brief and to the point.

After several attempts to get her to open up, Jo gave up. Her thoughts turned to the wallet and the missing man. Thank goodness, Gary was able to clear up the mystery of the unlocked cellar doors and the splotch of blood.

There was still the mystery of what happened to Carrie Ford. Could it be she experienced some sort of medical episode and didn't remember driving off the road? Still, she claimed someone from the farm followed her from the open house.

"We're here." Jo pulled into the store's parking lot and an empty parking spot near the back. "I hope you don't mind walking."

"Not at all. It's a nice day." They exited the vehicle. Michelle grabbed the stack of reusable grocery bags while Jo steered an empty shopping cart out of the cart corral.

Delta had given Jo a brand-specific grocery list, and it took the women over an hour to locate the exact items on Delta's list.

After they finished, the women loaded the bags of groceries in the back of the SUV before climbing inside and heading home.

Jo, determined to learn more about her resident, tried again. "So what's your favorite job on the farm?"

"I like keeping the women's common area neat and tidy." Michelle glanced at Jo. "Weird, huh?"

"No. I don't think it's weird."

"Cleaning makes me feel like I'm accomplishing something." Michelle tugged on her seatbelt. "I like to help Delta in the kitchen, too, but I feel like I'm all thumbs and in the way."

"I'm the same." Jo smiled. "That's Delta's personality. She rules the kitchen with an iron rolling pin."

"She does." Michelle grew quiet as she stared out the window.

"What would you like to do after you leave Divine and *Second Chance*?"

"I don't know."

Jo noticed Michelle clenching her fists in her lap. "You like cleaning. Perhaps you could find a job working as a hotel maid or open your own cleaning service."

"It's hard to land a gig with a rap sheet."

"Hard, but not impossible. Where there's a will, there's a way."

"Right." Michelle grew quiet again, and Jo sensed the woman's anxiety.

"You'll have plenty of time to sort it out," Jo said gently. "It wasn't a question to hint that you're leaving, but me just trying to give you some ideas for down the road."

"I know and thank you. I feel like such a failure. I've made so many bad choices in my life," Michelle sighed. "Like I'm afraid to make any decisions because I'm sure I'll screw it up again."

"Now that's where you're wrong." They reached the farm and Jo steered the SUV into the driveway. "I have faith in you, Michelle. I see your determination. If you have a true desire to change, you can conquer the world."

Jo parked the vehicle alongside the back of the house, next to the farm's pickup truck. "Looks like Delta made it back."

"Yes, ma'am." Michelle grabbed the door handle.

Jo reached across the seat to stop her. "I have an idea. I found an online site. It matches your personality to an ideal job. It looks kind of fun. In fact, I planned to try it myself. Would you like to try it, too?"

Michelle's eyes lit. "Really? Yes. I mean, yeah."

"Perfect. We'll pop into my office first thing tomorrow morning so you can take the test."

The women began unloading the back of the SUV, carrying the bags of groceries into the kitchen. Delta was nowhere in sight.

When they'd finished unloading the vehicle, there was still no sign of Jo's friend. "I wonder where Delta is hiding."

"Would you like me to try to find her?" Michelle asked.

"If you don't mind. I need to start putting some of this stuff away." Jo reached into an insulated recyclable bag and pulled out a gallon of milk.

"Not at all." Michelle darted out the back door while Jo buzzed around the kitchen.

Delta was a stickler for order and inventory, and Jo was certain she wasn't storing the items where her friend would want. She finished putting the last item in the fridge when Delta barged into the kitchen, her face red and out of breath.

"You look like you swallowed a gallon of Gary's homemade hot sauce."

"I wish that was all it was," Delta fumed. "We got a mess of trouble on our hands."

Chapter 8

"What kind of trouble?" Jo asked.

"I stopped by *Divine Delicatessen* on my way home to pick up one of Marlee's divine mile high lemon pies, and you'll never guess who I ran into."

"Debbie Holcomb."

"Close."

"Carrie."

"Debbie *and* Carrie. They were having lunch together. According to Marlee, Debbie was telling anyone and everyone who would listen that Nash tried to run Carrie off the road and you did something to poor Craig Grasmeyer."

"Sheriff Franklin and two investigators were here earlier with a search warrant. They searched the place and questioned the residents."

"Well, then they came up emptyhanded," Delta said.

"Not quite."

"What do you mean?"

"I mean while they were having a look around, Franklin discovered the cellar doors were unlocked and a splotch of blood on the cellar steps," Jo said.

"That was Gary's blood. He cut his hand when he was in the cellar checking out the canning supplies."

"I found that out after I called him. We still don't know how Grasmeyer's wallet ended up in our bathroom. Carrie claims a vehicle *similar* to our truck followed her from the open house and forced her off the road."

"Holcomb has Carrie convinced that it was Nash."

"She doesn't give up. I would like to drive right over to Holcomb's house and..."

"I'm right there with you, my friend," Delta said. "Maybe we can drop a box of special ex-lax brownies on her porch."

"Delta…"

"I'm kidding. You have to admit she's doing a good job of stirring things up."

"True. So now what?"

"We're going to spring a surprise visit on Carrie tomorrow morning and ply her with breakfast goodies. Maybe we can get to the bottom of what really happened after she left last night."

Despite her misgivings on surprising anyone with a visit, Jo finally agreed.

While Delta rearranged the groceries, Jo searched for the cellar padlock. She found it in the yard, near the corner of the house.

Jo replaced the lock and then returned to the kitchen to help Delta finish making dinner. While they cooked, Jo shared her concerns about Michelle and the woman's fear of failure.

"So we're going to take one of those online personality tests that match your personality to your ideal job tomorrow morning. I think it would be fun. You should take it, too."

"No need for me to take one of those tests." Delta waved her wooden spoon. "I'm doing exactly what the Good Lord wants me to do, other than maybe opening up a shooting range."

"Now that's an idea," Jo grinned. "You could open up a combination gun range and restaurant and call it *Guns and Good Eats*."

"I like it...*Guns and Good Eats*. Maybe we should rename *Divine Baked Goods Shop*."

"It's catchy. I'll give you that." Jo helped Delta set the table as the women began arriving for dinner. She took her place at the head of the table and noticed someone was missing. "Where's Nash?"

"Oh, I forgot to tell you. He won't be here for dinner. He went into town to buy some lumber for the workshop," Sherry said.

"I'll save him a plate of food," Delta said. "Nash will be heartbroken when he discovers he missed out on my stuffed meatloaf."

The women finished their dinner. They oohed and aahed over Marlee's delectable lemon pie, although they unanimously agreed the pie was a smidgen shy of tasting as amazing as Delta's desserts.

After dinner, the women pitched in to clean up while Jo decided to catch up on some paperwork. She set her cell phone on the corner of the desk and noticed there was a missed call. Jo unlocked the screen, and her heart skipped a beat when she discovered it was Sheriff Franklin.

There was no message, and she thought about returning the call but decided against it. Maybe she didn't want to know why he was calling.

Jo finished her paperwork and headed into the living room where she found Delta sprawled out in the recliner, a bowl of vanilla ice cream in her lap. "You look comfy."

"I'm beat. I'm too old to be scraping wallpaper. My feet are swelling and my back is giving me fits." Delta scooped up a large spoonful of ice cream. "My plan is to take a Motrin and head to bed as soon as *Wheel of Fortune* ends."

"I don't blame you. Scraping wallpaper isn't my idea of fun, either."

"Now don't forget about us stopping by Carrie's place tomorrow. I'm going to make a batch of cinnamon rolls to take with us."

"Your cinnamon rolls are delicious. I'll get up early to help." Jo patted Delta's shoulder on her way to the front porch.

Duke followed her out. "I wonder what goodies we'll find in the mailbox." Jo grabbed the mail and began sifting through the small stack on her way back to the porch when she heard tires on the gravel.

It was Nash. Instead of parking in his usual spot next to the workshop, he circled the drive and parked near the porch steps.

Jo knew the second she saw his face something was terribly wrong. She waited until he exited the truck. "Is everything all right?"

"No, Jo. Unfortunately, it's not."

"What is it?" Jo had a feeling that Nash's bad news was related to the call she'd missed from the sheriff.

"Craig Grasmeyer's jeep and body were found in the ditch only a couple of miles down the road from here."

The color drained from Jo's face. "You can't be serious."

"I'm dead serious. Looks like someone took him out."

"Someone murdered him?"

"Maybe. A lot of locals didn't care for him, and neither did I," Nash said. "I used to buy lumber from him for the workshop until he started selling me treated seconds, trying to pawn them off as quality wood. When I called him out, he threatened to sue me for defamation."

Jo began to pace. "The authorities have no proof we had anything to do with Grasmeyer's death."

"I wish it was that simple. They found Grasmeyer's cell phone in his vehicle. It appears that the last person he called was me."

Chapter 9

"You talked to him before he died?" Jo asked. "Did he say anything that struck you as odd, like perhaps he was concerned for his safety or someone was harassing him?"

"I never talked to him. He left a message on my phone." Nash told Jo how Grasmeyer left a message, offering to give him a special discount on a stack of lumber in his back storage shed.

"I'm sure you let the authorities listen to the message, and they cleared you from suspicion."

"Not so fast." Nash ran a ragged hand through his cropped locks. "They haven't cleared me - cleared us - of anything. There's still Carrie's claim someone followed her from the open house and the fact she found his wallet in our bathroom."

"What a mess." Jo absentmindedly patted Duke. "You should check the surveillance cameras, to see if there was any sign of Grasmeyer."

"I already did. There were so many people here; it was hard to make heads or tails of our guests. What if they start investigating us?" Nash asked. "Call me crazy, but what if one of Grasmeyer's enemies took him out, and used the open house as the perfect opportunity to set one of us up?"

"I thought I heard voices out here." Delta eased the screen door open and stepped onto the porch. "You missed my stuffed meatloaf."

"Sorry, Delta. I've had my hands full. The authorities found Craig Grasmeyer's body not far from here."

"No kidding." Delta limped to the railing. "What happened to him?"

"The cops aren't talking," Nash said.

He briefly told Delta what had transpired and she let out a low whistle. "Grasmeyer was not at the open house. I would bet my life on it. We searched this entire place."

"But his wallet was found here," Nash said. "I'm the last person Grasmeyer called."

"We know the truth," Delta said. "Don't you worry none. Jo and I are gonna chat with Carrie tomorrow morning. The woman causes more trouble with her tinkering around in other people's business than anyone else I know. For all we know, *she* planted the wallet and made up the story about someone following her."

Even though Delta and Jo attempted to reassure Nash the authorities would eventually clear him, Jo could tell the man's death was weighing heavy on his mind.

She waited until Nash climbed back inside the pickup truck and drove to the other side of the driveway before speaking. "This doesn't look good."

"No, it sure doesn't," Delta agreed. "Craig Grasmeyer was a crooked businessman with more than his share of enemies."

"Perhaps one of those enemies planned the perfect murder, making it look like someone else was responsible," Jo said.

"Based on the goings on around here since last night, it looks like that's what's happened." Delta shook her head. "Before we head to Carrie's place tomorrow, I think we should swing by *Divine Delicatessen* to find out what Marlee has heard about Grasmeyer's death."

Jo slipped her arm through Delta's. "Are you sure you weren't a crime scene investigator in a previous life?" she teased. "Maybe you should take the online personality test. If you ever get tired of cooking, you can take up catching criminals."

"I do love me a good mystery, but mostly I don't want to see one of my friends or anyone I care about on the hook for a crime they didn't commit. I hate to say it, but Franklin won't be looking too hard to find a culprit now."

"That's what I'm afraid of." Jo sucked in a breath. "Unfortunately, we already have one strike against us because of Gary's recent attack."

"We got a target on our back." Delta waited for Duke to trot inside before she turned off the porch light and followed Jo. "I have a feeling it's gonna be up to us to clear Nash's name."

Jo paused when they reached the bottom of the stairs. "I'll see you early tomorrow morning to help with the cinnamon rolls."

"Sounds good." Delta turned to go before turning back. "You're a good friend, Jo Pepperdine. We'll get through this like we have everything else."

"Yes, we will. One way or another." Jo wearily trudged up the stairs. It had been a long day, and she was ready for it to end.

As Jo got ready for bed, the events of the past twenty-four hours began running through her mind.

She was certain Nash was not responsible for Carrie's accident or Craig Grasmeyer's death, but the evidence against him was beginning to stack up.

An inkling of doubt crept into her mind. How much did she know about Nash Greyson other than he'd lived in the area for years, was divorced and had one son? She might not know much about the man's private life, but what she did know was that Nash was a strong and steady presence.

He had been instrumental in helping her get the farm ready for the new residents. He'd helped Jo out more than she could ever repay him for.

But that was the extent of it. She'd never bothered to run a background check on him before offering him a job and a place to live.

Was it possible Nash had a secret past? What if he had murdered Grasmeyer and accidentally left the man's wallet in the downstairs bathroom?

Maybe Nash was trying to make it look like Jo murdered the man. Jo mentally shook her head. It wasn't possible. There was no way Nash was a killer.

Despite her belief that Nash was not responsible for the recent events, she decided she would run a background check on her employee first thing tomorrow morning - just in case.

*****

"What are you doing?"

Jo clutched her chest and spun around in the chair. "You scared me half to death."

"Sorry." Delta wandered across the room and peered over Jo's shoulder.

"I'm doing a background check."

"On who? I thought you already checked out the new resident, Tara."

"It's on Nash."

"Nash?" Delta straightened. "Haven't you already done that?"

Jo wrinkled her nose.

"Joanna Pepperdine," Delta scolded. "Are you telling me you never ran a background check on Nash?"

"No. I mean, I didn't see the need. I didn't run one on you, either."

"Well, you ought to." Delta pulled up a chair and plopped down. "You need to run background checks on every single person before they move in."

"Everyone knows Nash."

"And everyone knows me, but safety and security come first. What did you find?"

"I'm still working on it." Jo's eyes squinted as she studied the screen. "Nash Greyson isn't a common name, but there are still a couple coming up in my search."

"There." Delta tapped her fingernail on the screen. "That's our Nash."

Jo clicked on the link, and Nash's file opened. She slowly scrolled the screen, searching for anything that appeared out of the ordinary.

"You're scrolling too fast," Delta said.

"I feel like I'm spying on him."

"Not spying...verifying as in verifying everything he told you is accurate. Hold up," Delta said. "I think I see something."

Jo released her grip on the mouse. "Where?"

"There."

"I don't..." Jo leaned in for a closer inspection. "Education, employment, credit history, criminal background and civil court records. What's this?" She clicked on the link labeled *Military Service Records*. "Did you know Nash was in the army?"

"I had no idea." Delta's eyes scanned the paragraph. "A twelve-year stint in the army. No wonder our hottie stays in such good shape."

"Delta." Jo shook her head. "Are you ogling Nash?"

"I don't ogle, I admire," Delta joked. "You know you've checked him out, too. We all have."

"Oh, brother." Jo clicked out of the military service screen and finished skimming the file. "I don't see anything that screams killer."

"Me, neither. Now look me up," Delta said. "I wanna know what kinda dirt that's out there on me."

"Should I be concerned?" Jo teased.

"Maybe. We'll find out soon enough." Delta rattled off her pertinent information while Jo tapped the computer keys. Delta's information popped up, and Jo clicked on the link.

"You're holding up pretty good for being in your early sixties."

Delta whacked her arm. "Not funny. Besides, the sixties are the new forties."

"Then I've got plenty of time." Jo sobered as she finished scrolling the screen. "You're as clean as a whistle."

"I guess they never recorded that armed robbery back in the eighties."

"Delta," Jo gasped.

"Kidding...I'm just kidding." Delta wiggled out of the chair and stood. "I need to get started on those cinnamon rolls. If we time it right, we'll be able to catch Carrie after church and before she heads out for bingo at the *American Legion*."

"I planned to attend the early service at the *Church of God* this morning, but after the day we had yesterday, I figured it would only draw more attention to me...to us."

"If you go into hiding, people will start to suspect you have a reason to hide."

"Speaking of church, why don't you ever go to church with me, Delta? You like Pastor Murphy."

"Because." Delta lowered her gaze and studied her feet.

"Because why?"

"I don't belong there. I don't fit in."

"How can you not 'fit in' at church?"

Delta's shoulders slumped. "We both know I'm a little rough around the edges, what with me working at the prison all of those years. I tend to say the wrong things sometimes and managed to maybe step on a few toes. God still loves me. I would rather watch a sermon on television or on my laptop."

"Someone said something to you in church," Jo guessed.

Michelle appeared in the doorway, interrupting the conversation. "I hope I'm not too early. I thought I would stop by in case Jo had time to run that personality test on me to see...you know, what I should do after I leave here."

Delta squeezed past Michelle and motioned for her to take her place. "You got plenty of time to make a decision, Michelle. I think Jo's been champing at the bit to give it a go, though."

"Are you sure this is a good time?" Michelle shrank back. "I can always come back later."

"Please." Jo patted the chair Delta vacated. "Have a seat. This will be fun."

Michelle slowly made her way across the room. She perched on the edge of the seat and absentmindedly tugged on her blouse. "Maybe I'm not going to be good at anything."

"Yes, you are," Jo said softly. "You're a good worker. I've never heard of a single complaint from customers at the mercantile or in the bakeshop."

"While you two work on the test, I'll get started on the cinnamon rolls." Delta slipped out of the office while Jo turned her attention to the computer screen.

She'd found several online personality tests and decided to try the one called the *Values Assessment Report*. There weren't many requirements, and the site promised fast results.

The test consisted of a set of twenty tiles. After reading the statements, the participant was instructed to drag and drop the tiles in various columns, based on the level of their importance...from least important to most important.

Michelle traded places with Jo. The woman studied the tiles and began placing them in the empty slots.

Jo waited for her to finish. "Our next step is to generate a report."

"It's probably going to tell me I'm not compatible for anything."

"That's nonsense." Jo waited for the report to populate and then leaned in. "It looks like you're an achiever."

Michelle read the results. "People who score high in the achievement cluster should look for jobs which let them use their best abilities. It's also important they look for work where they can see the results of their efforts directly. They should explore jobs where they get a strong feeling of accomplishment."

"See?" Jo tapped Michelle's arm. "This is exactly what you said. You like to clean the common area because it gives you a sense of accomplishment."

"Right."

"So let's find out what types of jobs best suit you." Jo pointed to the "next results" button.

The program generated a second report and Michelle's career matches. "Oh my gosh." Michelle's mouth dropped open. "This says I should be a mathematician or a statistician. I hate math."

"Me, too. What other career matches might be a good fit?" Jo rattled off the list while Michelle scrolled the screen. "What about a tailor or dressmaker? Those are both near the top of the matches."

"I've never sewed before. I do like working with my hands in Nash's shop. He's good at teaching stuff, too."

"He's a great guy." Jo thought of the other night, when she stopped by his apartment to question him about Carrie. She forced the image of Nash from her mind. "This confirms what you and I already suspected."

"Do you mind if I print this off, so I can take it back to the apartment and study it?" Michelle asked.

"Of course not." It took a few moments for Jo to figure out how to print the full report. After she did, she handed it to Michelle and stood. "That was fun. In fact, I think I'm going to suggest the other women take the test, too."

"Thanks, Jo." Michelle carefully folded the papers into thirds and tucked them in her back pocket. "I better head home to take a shower. I'm opening the bakeshop with Sherry today."

Michelle gave Delta a quick wave before hurrying out the back door.

Delta waited until the backdoor slammed behind her. "Well? What did you find out?"

"The assessment was interesting. Michelle is achievement motivated. She would do well to choose a job where she can see the results firsthand." Jo grabbed her apron off the hook and dropped it over her head. "Now put me to work."

The morning passed quickly as the residents stopped by to grab a bite to eat. Even though the women were encouraged to attend church with Jo, it wasn't a requirement.

Those who didn't hung out in their rooms or the common area. Because Sunday was a busy tourist day, the mercantile and bakeshop were open from one in the afternoon until six in the evening.

Delta decided to whip up an extra batch of cinnamon rolls, to sell in the store and treat the women.

Nash stopped by as Delta was pulling the last batch from the oven. Jo handed him one she had just finished frosting.

He took a big bite and closed his eyes, savoring the rich cream cheese frosting and warm melt-in-your-mouth roll. "With one of these rolls, you'll be able to convince Carrie to spill the beans on every single soul in Divine," Nash mumbled.

"That's the plan," Delta said. "First, we're gonna stop by the deli to see what Marlee has heard. She's bound to know something."

"Are you sure you two want to go through all of this trouble?" Nash reached for a second roll.

"This is no trouble at all," Delta said. "My gut tells me there's more to Carrie's claims than meets the eye. The nosy-body has more dirt on the residents of Divine than the rest of us put together."

"I owe you one." Nash thanked the women and headed out, passing by Raylene who was on her way in. "Sherry told me y'all are heading into town to chat with Carrie, the woman who claims someone ran her off the road."

"And the one who found the dead guy's wallet in our bathroom," Jo said.

"Dead guy?" Raylene's eyes blinked rapidly. "Did I miss something?"

Delta explained how the authorities attempted to track Craig Grasmeyer down to return his wallet. "They found his jeep and his body not far from here."

"I think it's a setup." Jo set the tray of cinnamon rolls on the counter. "The authorities also found the man's cell phone in his vehicle. His last call was to Nash."

"And something leads me to believe Carrie Ford is somehow involved. There are too many coincidences." Delta placed a clear plastic lid on top of the cinnamon rolls and ran her thumb along the metal rim to seal it. "You got a nose for snooping around, why don't you tag along with Jo and me?"

"Are you serious?" Raylene clapped her hands.

"Why not? Three heads are better than one." Jo quickly warmed to the idea. "You have a good eye for detail, things Delta and I might miss."

"I also have an extremely accurate baloney radar, if I do say so myself."

"Perfect." Jo snapped her fingers. "Will you need to switch shifts with one of the other women?"

"Nope, as long as we're back here before three o'clock when I start my shift at the mercantile."

Jo ran into her office to grab the SUV keys and her purse. She met Raylene and Delta out back and tossed the keys to Raylene. "You drive."

"Me?" Raylene squeaked.

"Yep. I planned for you to take a refresher course and drive around the farm. If you drive to town, I can tick it off my to-do list."

"Are you sure?" Raylene stared at the keys in her hand. "What if we crash?"

"It's insured." Jo ran around to the passenger side before Raylene could refuse. "Besides, we won't be driving very fast or very far."

Delta placed the container of cinnamon rolls on the back seat before climbing in and reaching for the seatbelt. "Angels didn't save your life just so you could take the three of us out on a country backroad."

"You have a lot more faith in me than I do." Raylene settled in behind the wheel and pulled the door shut. "I don't see an ignition key."

"You don't need one." Jo explained how to turn the vehicle on by pressing the button on the dash.

Raylene followed Jo's instructions and fired up the engine. "Check that out. So what happens if you need a key?"

"It's hidden inside the key fob." Jo showed Raylene the hidden key.

"That's nifty."

Jo reviewed the basics while Raylene listened carefully. "Here goes nothing." She consulted the rearview mirror as she shifted into reverse.

Delta and Jo grew silent, allowing Raylene time to concentrate as she navigated the vehicle onto the road.

"You're doing great," Jo said. "See? Driving is a piece of cake."

"It's not as bad as I thought." Raylene relaxed her grip on the steering wheel.

While they rode, the women chatted about life on the farm and then the conversation drifted to Craig Grasmeyer's death. "Before we head to Carrie's place, we're gonna swing by *Divine Delicatessen* to see what Marlee may have heard."

When they reached Main Street and the restaurant, Raylene cautiously pulled the SUV into an empty spot and shifted into park.

Delta opened the door. "You stay here. I'll see if Marlee is around." She closed the door behind her and disappeared inside.

She was gone for several minutes before finally emerging, her expression anxious. "Marlee is here. She asked us to pull around back. She has something important to tell us."

Chapter 10

"Why not just go in the front door?" Jo asked.

"Too many nosy posies."

"I see." Jo didn't really see, but if Delta thought it was important they park out back, she knew the area residents better than Jo did.

Raylene drove to the other side of the building, along a small strip of gravel until they reached the back of the deli.

Marlee was waiting near the rear door. "Great minds think alike. I was going to call Delta on my first break. News about Craig Grasmeyer's death is spreading like wildfire."

"I'm sure," Jo groaned. "And I'm sure they're all talking about how his body was found not far from the farm."

"Yep," Marlee nodded. "I wouldn't worry much about that. Most of the people around here couldn't stand him. He was as corrupt as they come. Didn't help that his brother, a local judge, tended to let anything involving his brother slide."

"Really?" Jo lifted a brow. "We have one corrupt brother, and the other is a judge."

"Which means they were both corrupt," Delta quipped.

"Quite possibly," Marlee said. "I've been thinking about his death ever since Claire Harcourt stopped by first thing this morning. She heard they found Craig's body in a ditch outside of town. I also heard his gun and his Rolex watch are both missing. He never took the Rolex off...ever and now it's gone."

"A souvenir for the killer?" Jo mused.

"Could be."

The clatter of pans echoed from the restaurant's kitchen, and Marlee shifted away from the door. "I was thinking to myself, 'Marlee, who here in town would want to see Craig Grasmeyer dead?' Well, the list is growing."

"Like who?" Delta asked.

"It would be easier to tell you who didn't have it in for him." Marlee lifted a finger. "First of all, there's Wayne Malton who owns the hardware store. Craig did his best to drive poor Wayne and Charlotte out of business. Then there's Jesse, the postmaster. Craig tried for years to get his wife that job. He was constantly filing complaints against Jesse. Last I heard, Craig was bragging about an inside connection and how his wife was a shoo-in for the job, right before they split."

"My vote goes to Jesse McDougall," Jo said. "He could kill two birds with one stone...murder his wife's competition and throw us under the bus."

"True." Raylene, who so far remained silent, spoke. "So we have two solid suspects...the owner of the hardware store and the postmaster."

"Maybe more," Marlee said. "I think it would be worth it to take a closer look at Vicki Talbot."

"Who is Vicki Talbot?"

"Vicki is Divine's fashionista and Grasmeyer's employee. She's also the one who told the authorities she couldn't reach him but waited two days, until they showed up on the doorstep of his lumberyard, to mention it."

"Our list of suspects is growing by the minute," Jo said. "I need to start taking notes."

"I beat you to it." Marlee handed Jo a guest check. "I already jotted the names down so I wouldn't forget. I also added Craig's wife, Laurie, to the list."

"I've met her once or twice." Delta made a slicing motion across her neck. "I heard she has a terrible temper."

"We're up to four suspects and three with motive." Raylene lightly tapped her chin. "I'm still leaning toward the woman who was at the open house the other night, Carrie what's-her-name. The fact she was the one who found Grasmeyer's wallet and then conveniently claimed someone forced her off the road on her way home, insinuating she thought it was Nash. Something smells fishy."

"It was no secret Nash and Craig couldn't stand each other," Marlee said. "In fact, I think it's a perfect frame job. What better way to lead investigators in the wrong direction than to drop clues at an open house almost all of the area residents are attending?"

"Which also happens to be a home for former convicts." Delta turned to Raylene. "No offense."

"None taken," Raylene shrugged. "It's a fact. So a clever killer placed a clue at the open house and then forced a local off the road after leaving our place. All of the evidence points to someone who lives at *Second Chance*. It's basically brilliant."

"And one hundred percent a setup," Jo said. "You mentioned something about Grasmeyer and his wife splitting."

"Yep," Marlee nodded. "She finally got fed up with his shenanigans. Laurie may have an airtight alibi. She's been staying with her sister in another city."

"We still don't know how Grasmeyer died," Delta said. "Perhaps his death was accidental."

"I thought the same thing, until old loose lips, Evelyn McBride, spilled the beans. She said Grasmeyer was shot in the back of the head."

"Who is Evelyn McBride?" Raylene asked.

"Smith County Dispatch," Delta and Marlee said in unison.

"Hey, Marlee." A man appeared in the doorway. "We ran out of the breakfast specials."

"We better let you get back to work," Jo said. "Thank you for the information."

"You're welcome." Marlee hurried to the door. "I hope you get to the bottom of what happened. I have a feeling if the authorities determine someone took Grasmeyer out, they aren't going to look too far for Craig's killer if you know what I mean."

Before the trio could answer, she slipped back inside and the door shut.

Jo glanced at Marlee's handwritten notes. "The wife, the competitor and the postmaster. This is an interesting group of suspects."

"And maybe even the employee. I'm wondering why Vicki didn't contact the authorities if she thought her boss was missing," Delta said. "This list is a good start. Now, it's time to chat with Carrie."

Raylene consulted her watch. "It's forty minutes past ten."

"Church is letting out. I'm sure Carrie is on her way home, and we're going to be on her doorstep to greet her."

Delta took over driving, and they headed to the outskirts of town, an area Jo had never visited before and never even knew existed. They turned onto an unpaved side street, riddled with ruts.

The SUV jostled along.

Jo touched her temple. "This is a terrible road. How much farther before we get there?"

"We're close now." Delta maneuvered the vehicle to the edge of the road, and the jostling stopped. She turned onto a paved cul-de-sac and drove past several meticulously manicured estates.

"What's a nice development like this doing off a dirt road?"

"It's where the wealthy cheapskates live. Last I heard, they didn't want to pay to pave the road, plus they claim it deters the riff-raff or in other words, us lowly peasants." Delta turned onto *Serenity Lane* and pulled into the second drive.

Whatever Jo thought Carrie Ford's house might look like, this wasn't it. "This…is Carrie's place?" She stared at the whimsical cotton candy pink shutters and bright yellow siding.

"I take it they don't enforce HOA rules," Raylene laughed.

"Not in this neck of the woods. These folks make the rules, or at the very least are accustomed to bending them." Delta climbed out of the SUV and waited for the other two to join her near the front. "If you think the outside is a kaleidoscope of colors, wait until you see the inside."

"I can't wait." Jo followed Delta and Raylene up the sidewalk, lined with red and white striped candy canes. There was a soup spoon wind chime near the porch. Linking the spoons were round pieces of metal that reminded Jo of washers. "Carrie has some interesting artwork."

Delta pressed the doorbell. *Cuckoo, cuckoo, cuckoo.*

Jo burst out laughing. "A cuckoo doorbell chime? I think I've heard it all."

Carrie didn't answer, so Delta tried again. "She might not be home from church yet." She eased past Raylene and Jo and made her way to the garage door where she peered in the glass pane.

"Her van is here. Maybe she's around back and can't hear the doorbell." Delta walked past the garage door and disappeared from sight.

"Let's go." Raylene tugged on Jo's arm, and they followed Delta around the side of the house.

Jo abruptly stopped when they reached the backyard. It was a maze of bushes, adorned with more whimsical yard art. A stone path zigzagged back and forth, leading past a ceramic birdbath and tiered fountain.

They caught up with Delta, who stood on the back deck rapping lightly on the sliding glass door.

"Maybe she rode to church with someone else," Raylene suggested.

Delta shaded her eyes and peered through the glass. "So much for our element of surprise."

"We could hang around out front and wait for her to show up," Jo said.

Raylene wandered to the edge of the deck. "Hold on! Over here." She sprang from the deck and jogged past a hedge before coming to an abrupt halt.

"What on earth?"

Chapter 11

"What is it?" Jo caught up with Raylene and Delta.

"It's Carrie."

They found the woman sprawled out on a hammock; a slice of cucumber covering each of her eyes and a set of ear buds firmly wedged in each ear.

"Is she all right?" Jo whispered.

"I hope so." Raylene pointed to a bright red splotch on the front of Carrie's blouse. "We should check for a pulse." She reached for the woman's wrist.

Carrie bolted upright, the cucumbers plopping into her lap. "What...what's going on?"

"I'm sorry." Raylene snatched her hand back. "We thought you were hurt."

"With cucumbers covering my eyes and ear buds in my ears?"

"And blood on your shirt." Jo pointed to the splotch near her neckline.

"Huh?" Carrie lifted her shirt and inspected the stain. "That's catsup. I must've dribbled a little on me earlier while I was eating my hash browns." She tossed the cucumbers into the bushes and swung her legs over the side of the hammock.

"Between the cops showing up on my doorstep before daylight this morning and now you sneaking up on me, scaring me half to death, I'll never catch up on my beauty rest."

"Why were the cops on your doorstep this morning?" Delta asked.

"You haven't heard." Carrie held out a hand, and Jo pulled her off the hammock.

"About Craig Grasmeyer's death," Raylene said.

"Yep. Though I have my doubts he's dead," Carrie said.

"They found his body." Jo released her grip as soon as Carrie was on her feet. "Marlee heard he was shot in the back of the head."

"I won't believe it until I see a body," Carrie insisted. "Either he's alive, or there's someone sneaking around inside his house."

"How do you know?" Delta shifted to the side to make room for Carrie.

"Don't tell me you drove to his house to snoop on him, too," Jo said.

Carrie's face tightened. "I did not snoop. I was out walking Mr. Whipple last night and noticed someone standing by the window."

The woman fanned her face. "It's getting hot out here. Let's go inside." She didn't wait for an answer as she plodded past them and made her way toward the back of the house. "I have a fresh batch of sweet raspberry tea."

"Tea sounds good." Delta snapped her fingers. "Which reminds me. I have a surprise for you. I'll be right back."

Raylene and Jo followed Carrie inside while Delta headed to the SUV to grab the container of cinnamon rolls. By the time she joined them, Carrie had poured several glasses of tea.

"Ohhh...your cinnamon rolls look dee-licious." Carrie's eyes narrowed. "You didn't drive all the way over here just to bring me cinnamon rolls."

"We were hoping to talk to you about the incident the other night when you left the open house."

"Someone followed me from your place and forced my van off the road." Carrie reached for a cinnamon roll. "I could've sworn it was a pickup truck, similar to yours."

"But you're not one hundred percent certain." Raylene sipped her tea, eyeing Carrie over the rim of her glass.

"It sure looked like it."

"It was nighttime, and there's a chance it was someone else," Jo insisted.

"I suppose it could have been." Carrie took a big bite of the roll. A chunk of frosting dribbled down her chin. "Delta, these are to die for…not literally, of course."

"Thank you. Let's talk about you finding Craig Grasmeyer's wallet in the guest bathroom," Delta said.

"That's easy. When I got to your place, I took the tour with one of the residents. I think her name was Kelli. She was very nice, very polite. I was surprised considering the woman is a convicted felon."

"Who served her time and paid her dues," Jo pointed out.

"Right. Well…I finished the tour and headed inside because I was feeling a little dizzy. I drank some of the lemonade, which by the way was delicious." Carrie smacked her lips. "I need to get the recipe from you. I'm hosting the weekly bridge game on Wednesday and was thinking your lemonade along with my sugar cookies would make my bridge gals green with envy."

"Back to the open house," Raylene said. "You drank some lemonade and then what happened?"

"I needed to use the bathroom. It took me a couple of minutes to find it. Your house is a little choppy, and there are a lot of small rooms. It reminds me of the *Winchester Mystery House* out in California. You ever been there?" Carrie shivered. "Talk about small, haunted rooms."

"No, I've never been there," Jo said. "So you finally found the bathroom."

"Yes. After I finished tinkling, I washed my hands. That's when I saw it sitting on the bathroom windowsill."

"The wallet," Delta prompted.

"The wallet. I grabbed it and then went to find someone. I think her name was Sherry. We stopped Delta first, and then Sherry went to find you. Which is when you opened it up, and we discovered the wallet belonged to Craig Grasmeyer." Carrie waved the roll in Jo's direction.

"But Grasmeyer was never at the open house," Jo said. "We searched the place. No one remembers seeing him. Nash checked our surveillance cameras. There was no sign of the man."

"It's a mystery," Carrie cast Raylene a quick look. "I'm sure the authorities will want to question your...residents."

"It's a setup." Jo clenched her jaw. "Someone at the open house murdered Grasmeyer and then planted his wallet in my bathroom to make it look like he was there."

"Let's talk about the incident, where you said someone followed you from the open house and forced your van off the road," Delta said. "Tell us everything that happened from the moment Nash walked you to your vehicle."

"Well." Carrie's expression clouded. "I remember I was still feeling a little lightheaded. It could be the new anti-anxiety medication I'm taking. Nash offered to walk me out. I remember him helping me into my van, and then he left. I sat there for a few minutes, making sure I had my cell phone in my purse and whatnot. I circled around and pulled to the end of the driveway. Someone pulled up right behind me."

"And you think it was a pickup truck," Raylene prompted.

"I'm almost certain." Even though Carrie's voice was firm, Jo wasn't convinced judging by the look on her face.

"What does your insurance company say about your accident?" Delta reached for her glass of tea.

"I wasn't ticketed, and it's a good thing. I can't afford to have my insurance rates go up. I'm thinking about early retirement and need to watch my pennies because I'll be living on a fixed income." Carrie shoved the last of the roll into her mouth and licked her fingers. "My cousin took a look at the dent. He thinks he can pop it out, so I don't think I'll have to file a claim."

"Is that all that you remember?"

"Yep." Carrie nodded. "I found the wallet; left the open house and someone bumped the back of my van. I lost control, and then they took off."

"You said you're considering retirement?" Jo envisioned a bank teller or receptionist.

"Semi-retirement. I'm thinking of starting a small business...taxidermy. It was actually Abner, my most recent husband's business. I was his assistant."

"Taxidermy? Raylene snorted. "That's an interesting career."

"Oh, yes." Carrie nodded enthusiastically. "I was Abner's best customer." She leaned in and lowered her voice. "The first few months of our marriage, we were madly in love. The honeymoon didn't last long."

"I see." Jo, at a loss for words, sipped her tea.

"I gave up on men after Abner. It's hard, going to funerals every couple of years or so."

Jo spewed her mouthful of tea. "I'm sorry for your losses."

Carrie reached for another cinnamon roll. "Besides, it's slim pickings in Smith County. If I was in the market for another husband, I would have to start looking in Kansas City."

"You could try one of those online dating sites," Jo suggested.

"No way. They're full of cheaters and money grubbers." Carrie inhaled the cinnamon roll. "I'm pretty sure the authorities plan to search Craig Grasmeyer's property. I know for a fact I saw someone inside his place last night, which doesn't line up with the sheriff's insistence he's been dead and lying in the ditch for the past couple of days."

"Are you sure it wasn't someone else?" Delta asked. "Inside his house, I mean. Maybe you saw someone other than Craig Grasmeyer inside the house."

Carrie tapped her chin thoughtfully. "I was in close enough proximity to see the outline of the person. It sure looked like Grasmeyer to me."

A yellow and white cat stalked into the kitchen, dragging a small leash clamped firmly between his teeth. He dropped the leash next to Carrie's chair.

"Now here's the real troublemaker. Mr. Whipple kept me up, too. He was hearing noises outside. My motion light kept turning on, but when I went to look, there was no one there."

"Your cat was hearing noises?" Delta asked.

"Yeah. You know how dogs bark? Not Mr. Whipple. He starts yowling, almost as if he's in pain. He's been doing it since he was a kitten. He thinks he's part dog." Carrie bent down and scooped him up. "I take it you're ready for your morning walk."

Raylene chuckled. "You walk your cat?"

"Of course." Carrie scratched the cat's chin. "We walk every day - morning and night. I haven't gotten around to it today, what with me barely getting any sleep last night."

A sudden thought popped into Jo's head, and she stood. "Do you mind if we take a walk with you and...Mr. Whipple?"

Delta, realizing where Jo was going with her question, quickly chimed in. "We'll take a stroll past Grasmeyer's place and you can show us exactly where you were standing last night when you noticed someone inside."

"Yes. Yes, that will work. I need to change into my walking shoes." Carrie set the cat on the floor and disappeared down the hall.

Jo knelt down and patted the cat's head. "Mr. Whipple, you're a pretty kitty even if you're a little odd."

The yellow tabby yawned and then flopped over.

Carrie returned clad in an entirely different outfit.

Delta whistled. "Good heavens, Carrie. What in the world are you wearing?"

"Exercise weights. These work great for keeping me slim and trim." Carrie pirouetted in a small circle, revealing a black band of Velcro and a row of rubber sticks. "I gave up on wearing the thigh weights. They kept falling off."

Carrie extended her left leg. "The ankle weights work just fine."

"Now for you. We're going to have company today. Isn't that nice?" The woman shifted her ample frame and clipped the leash to the cat's gem-studded collar. "I'll grab a can of cat food and some water for Bugsy, and we'll be on our way."

"Bugsy?"

"Grasmeyer's cat. I've been feeding him for weeks now, ever since Laurie left." Carrie grabbed a bottled water from the fridge and a can of cat food from the cupboard before leading Mr. Whipple to the door. "Mr. Whipple and Bugsy are buddies."

Delta, Raylene and Jo followed Carrie and the cat down the steps. They strolled to the end of the drive and turned onto the sidewalk.

The neighborhood was peaceful and picturesque with towering oak trees lining the streets that shaded the meticulously manicured lawns.

The mostly two-story Tudor homes sat back from the street, with long meandering driveways leading to oversized garages. Parked in the drives were an array of high-end SUVs and luxury sports cars.

"So this is where the money is," Raylene said.

"This is where the money lives." Carrie drifted from side to side as Mr. Whipple stopped to inspect the grass and anything else that caught his eye. "I bought my place right after Abner and I married. No way was I going to live in the dump he called home."

When they reached the end of the street, the women turned right onto another cul-de-sac. This street sported homes with even larger lawns. Ornate wrought iron fences surrounded the properties. Electric gates guarded the long brick drives and the stately homes behind them.

The cat picked up the pace and Carrie hurried after him. "Mr. Whipple gets excited when we get close to Bugsy's home." The cat leaped between a pair of iron spindles causing Carrie, who was balancing the can of cat food and water in her other hand, to lose her grip on the leash.

Mr. Whipple never looked back as he sprinted down the driveway. "You stinker!" Carrie shouted. "You know you're not supposed to run off."

"I hope he comes back." Delta peered through the spindles.

"He won't." Carrie set her things on the sidewalk and began punching the buttons on the gate's keypad. "We'll have to go in after him."

The gate made a faint whirring noise and then slowly opened.

"Craig Grasmeyer gave you the code to his security gate?" Jo gasped.

"Not quite." Carrie picked up the food and water. "I figured it out on my own. It only took me a couple of tries. Most people pick easy codes, like one, two, three or four, or all ones or some such thing. Grasmeyer put a little more thought into his."

"And you were able to crack the code," Raylene said.

"Yep. It's 16076."

"That's random."

"Not really." Carrie motioned to the numbers on the front of the house. "He used his house number for his gate code."

"Ah." Jo lifted a brow. "So you regularly access his property."

"Not regularly. Only when Mr. Whipple manages to escape, and he runs off." Carrie pointed to the sidewalk. "Last night, I was standing right here, trying to coax him out. I was getting ready to open the gate and go after him when I noticed a shadow crossing back and forth in the upstairs windows. I figured it was Grasmeyer."

Jo studied the second story. "Which windows?"

"The windows above the garage. Those are the master bedroom windows," Carrie explained.

"You've been inside Grasmeyer's place?" Delta's eyes squinted.

"I was inside years ago when it was for sale before Grasmeyer and his wife bought it." Carrie strolled up the drive.

Jo hurried to keep up. "We're trespassing."

"True. But then who's here to report us? Marlee told me yesterday that Laurie is staying with her sister in Wichita. I'm sure she'll be coming back to settle the affairs."

"She could be on her way here now. You said the authorities planned to search the property," Raylene said.

"Which means we stand a chance of being caught trespassing," Delta pointed out.

"Not if we hurry." Carrie peeled the lid off the can of cat food and set it next to the garage. "I left a water dish around here somewhere." She stuck her hand inside the shrub. "Ah, there it is."

Carrie pulled out a small plastic bowl, set it next to the can of cat food and poured water into the dish. "I'm sure Mr. Whipple is around back. We'll have to go get him. At least he can't get inside the pool enclosure. He doesn't know how to swim."

She finished filling the water dish, and then led them around the side of the house. On the right was a six-foot privacy fence. A row of overgrown shrubbery ran along the front. "There's way too much shrubbery along the front and side of the house. Overgrown shrubbery is an ideal cover for robbers."

161

"Or killers," Jo said.

The backyard was small, or maybe it just looked small. It sported an in-ground lap pool surrounded by a two-story screen enclosure, along with a fire pit and built-in gas grill.

Several wooden Adirondack chairs circled the fire pit. Propped up against one of the chairs were several metal roasting sticks.

Delta picked up one of the sticks. "Looks like there was a party going on back here."

"Right?" Jo studied the chairs and then took a step closer, peering into the fire pit.

Raylene slipped in next to Jo. She placed a light hand over the top of the pit before picking up one of the charred embers. "These embers are stone cold. Whoever had the bonfire didn't do it last night. Embers retain heat for up to twenty-four hours."

"I didn't notice a bonfire last night. Here kitty, kitty," Carrie sing-songed. "Where are you, Mr.

Whipple?" She parted the bushes lining the brick wall. "Come out you little stinker."

Meow.

"I think I hear him." Carrie dove behind the bushes.

"Do you need some help?" Jo asked.

"No." Carrie's muffled voice echoed out. "Listen, mister...I am *not* messing around."

There was another meow, but it wasn't coming from the bushes. It was coming from the screen enclosure.

"Mr. Whipple is inside the pool enclosure," Raylene pointed to the cat, hovering in the far corner.

"Are you sure?" A disheveled Carrie emerged, a broken twig sticking out of her hair. "There must be a hole in the screen. I'm afraid this place is going to go downhill now that Grasmeyer is dead, and it will hurt our property values."

The women spread out, each searching for the opening in the screen where Mr. Whipple managed to sneak in.

"I found it." Raylene nudged one of the screen door panels with her foot. "The cat must've gone in through here."

Carrie hurried over. "Sure enough."

"Now what?" Delta peered through the screen. "I see him over in the corner. His leash is wrapped around a potted plant."

"Great. The numbskull is going to end up choking himself." Carrie dropped to her knees. "Unfortunately, my cat leaves me no other choice. I'm going in."

Chapter 12

Carrie pushed the panel out and crawled through the opening.

"You're gonna have to suck it in." Raylene knelt down to help guide Carrie. "You're almost there and...bingo."

"Crazy cat." Carrie placed a hand on the wall and slowly stood. "I don't know why I put up with his shenanigans. I should leave him here to find his own way out." She circled the pool, stair stepping over the waterfall platform in the back.

Mr. Whipple eyed his human with interest as she untangled his leash. "You are so naughty. If you don't knock it off, we're not going to come back here anymore to visit Bugsy. In fact, we're going straight home. No visit for you today."

Mr. Whipple squirmed back and forth in an attempt to escape Carrie's hold. She returned to the point of entry and placed him on the cement pad, keeping a tight grip on him.

"I'll hang onto Mr. Whipple." Delta took the leash from Carrie while Raylene helped her exit the enclosure.

"What are we gonna do about the popped panel?" Jo asked.

"Not much we can do," Carrie said.

"Shhh." Delta pressed a finger to her lips. "Do you hear that? I thought I heard voices."

"I heard it, too," Jo whispered. This time, there was no mistaking a male voice, coming from the front of the property.

"We gotta hide." Carrie scooped Mr. Whipple up and jogged to the wall of shrubs. She shielded her cat with both hands and dove for cover.

Jo hesitated for a fraction of a second before squeezing through the narrow opening, joining Carrie on the other side.

Delta and Raylene weren't far behind. The four women huddled close together, as Jo attempted to peer out.

She strained to hear the male voice again, but it was quiet. Jo inched to the right, to give Raylene who was next to her some breathing room. A sharp twig stabbed her in the arm. "Ouch."

"Shh." Delta clamped a hand over Jo's mouth, and she frowned.

"...and Laurie Grasmeyer will be here shortly to let us inside."

"You don't think she's responsible, do you?" Jo recognized Deputy Brian Franklin's voice, and she caught a glimpse of a side profile as he and another man Jo had never seen before strolled past the bushes, mere inches from where the women were hiding.

Jo squeezed her eyes shut, praying the deputy and his companion would keep moving.

The men circled the enclosure and disappeared around the other side of the property.

Jo swatted Delta's hand away from her mouth. "We've got to get out of here. If we get caught, Franklin is going to throw us in jail."

"For what? Trespassing?" Delta shook her head. "Or hiding behind bushes?"

"Fine. Maybe not arrest us, but he'll for sure haul us down to the sheriff's department to question us. This doesn't look good."

"I have to agree," Raylene said calmly. "Unless we can find another way out, we're trapped until the authorities finish searching the house."

"And...and the grounds," Carrie stammered. "I've never been incarcerated." She turned to Raylene, her eyes as round as saucers. "I heard the body searches are rough."

"We're not going to jail." Delta rolled her eyes. "There has to be another way out of here." She pressed her body against the cold concrete wall and slowly made her way toward the front of the property.

Their options were limited...they needed to try to find another way out or risk revealing their hiding spot. Jo opted to find another way out and joined Delta to help search for a possible escape.

Carrie shifted Mr. Whipple to her other hand and cleared the bushes, stepping out into the yard.

"What are you doing?" Raylene hissed.

"I'm going out the way I came in. I'll just explain to the deputy that Mr. Whipple got loose and I came back here to get him."

"Way to leave us high and dry."

"I'm not leaving you high and dry. I'm going to create a diversion on the other side of the garage so that nice Deputy Franklin and his companion will come to my aid. While I'm doing that, you make a run for it. Stick to the left-hand side of the property. There's a gap between the fence and the cement wall near the front."

"What if your diversion doesn't work?" Jo whispered.

"Do you have a better idea?"

"Good point." Delta gave Carrie a thumbs up and continued her slow trek to the front. The trio crept forward for several more feet before reaching the end of the shrubs. They would have to trust Carrie to follow through with her promise to create a diversion while they made a run for it.

Delta held the bushes back while Jo and Raylene climbed out.

"Do you see anyone?" Delta whispered.

"Nope. The coast is clear."

"Let's go." Raylene gave Jo a gentle nudge and then sprinted across the yard. Delta and Jo were hot on her heels. The women didn't slow until they reached the corner.

Sure enough, there was a small gap. Raylene easily squeezed between the wall and the fence. Delta was next. She made it halfway through when her girth stopped her. "I'm stuck."

"Y-you can't be stuck," Jo's voice cracked. "You have to get through. Suck it in, and I'll give you a push."

Delta's face turned beet red. She nodded her head and sucked in a breath. Jo pushed while Raylene pulled from the other side.

"Just a little more." Jo placed both hands on Delta's arm and pushed as hard as she could, giving her friend the momentum she needed to clear the opening.

Jo didn't look back as she eased through the gap and onto the sidewalk out front. "We made it."

"That was fun. Not." Delta lifted the front of her shirt, revealing several angry scratches across her midsection.

"I'm sorry," Jo apologized. "I guess we should've come clean and fessed up to the deputy we were snooping."

"And miss out on all of this fun?" Delta asked sarcastically.

"I'm sorry, too," Raylene apologized.

"Stop apologizing," Delta said. "It's just a few minor scrapes. We better keep moving in case Laurie Grasmeyer shows up and wonders what we're doing."

The women walked in silence, making their way back to Carrie's place. There was no sign of Carrie, and Jo hoped the authorities believed the woman's story about the cat, which was technically the truth.

"Should we leave?" Raylene asked.

"No. We need to wait for Carrie," Jo said.

"Maybe we should try her cell phone," Delta suggested.

"Hang on." Raylene motioned to the street and a patrol car heading toward them. It circled the cul-de-sac before stopping in front of Carrie's driveway.

Deputy Franklin exited the driver's side. He opened the back door and helped Carrie, who was holding Mr. Whipple, from the vehicle.

She limped toward them. The deputy trailed behind.

"Hello, Delta, Jo. What are you doing here?"

"We...uh." Jo shot Delta a quick glance.

"We brought you some cinnamon rolls. We thought you weren't home and were getting ready to leave," Delta said. "Are you all right?"

"Yes. I'm fine. I had a minor mishap. As luck would have it, Deputy Franklin happened to be in the area and came to my aid." Carrie smiled brilliantly at the deputy. "If not for him, I would still be lying on the ground."

"You might want to consider carrying your cell phone with you when you're out walking," the deputy said.

"I will from now on. This was definitely a wakeup call." Carrie patted the deputy's arm. "I can't always depend on the local authorities to be around to rescue me."

With a nod to Delta, Raylene and Jo, the deputy returned to his car and slowly drove off.

Carrie set her cat on the grass and began limping toward her house. Jo fell into step. "I thought you were faking it. Are you sure you're all right?"

"Yeah. Dummy me was going to fake a fall but managed to pull off the real deal. Grasmeyer needs to do something about the potholes in his yard."

"It's Laurie's problem now," Delta said. "Thanks for taking the fall...literally."

"Haha," Carrie muttered. "You're welcome."

"Delta was injured, too," Raylene said.

"I scraped a chunk of fat off the old tummy," Delta said. "All for nothing."

"Oh, it wasn't all for nothing," Carrie said. "Deputy Franklin told me they were close to making an arrest in Grasmeyer's death."

"Did he mention any names?" Jo immediately thought of Nash.

"Nope. I tried to get him to spill the beans, but he was tight-lipped."

Carrie continued. "The investigators must think they're onto something. They're searching for some sort of clue. I wish I knew who it was I saw inside that house last night."

"You said earlier, you thought it was a male," Raylene said.

"I did?" Carrie blinked rapidly. "I don't recall mentioning it was a male. I saw an outline of someone and thought it was Grasmeyer, but that was before I found out he was dead."

"Carrie." Delta forced herself to remain calm. "You told us earlier you could've sworn you saw Craig Grasmeyer in his upstairs bedroom last night."

"Are you sure?" Carrie rubbed her brow. "I'm getting confused."

"So maybe you didn't see anyone inside his house last night," Jo said.

A blank expression crossed Carrie's face. "Right, but one thing is certain. Well...two...the investigators are close to making an arrest, and they're searching his place for a reason. I really need to talk to the doctor about the new anti-anxiety medication I'm on. It's whacking me out."

"What's that?" Delta pointed to something white sticking out of Carrie's blouse.

"What's what?"

"It looks like a piece of paper sticking out of the top of your blouse."

"Paper?" Carrie patted her blouse. "It's uh...my mail. I grabbed it earlier."

"Earlier before we took Mr. Whipple for a walk?" Now Jo was getting confused.

"No. After that nice Deputy Franklin dropped me off."

"We watched you get out of his patrol car. You didn't grab your mail," Delta patiently explained.

"Let's see." Jo held out her hand.

"Why?" Carrie took a step back.

"Because something fishy is going on." Jo snapped her fingers. "Mail please."

"Fine." Carrie dropped the mail in Jo's hand.

Jo glanced at the envelope. "This is Grasmeyer's mail."

"I thought we might find something important," Carrie said. "Like a clue."

"Tampering with the US mail is a felony," Delta said.

"A felony? I'm just borrowing it." A look of panic crossed Carrie's face. "On second thought, I'm going to throw it in the trash."

"Don't you want to see what it is?" Delta asked. "You went to all of the trouble to steal it."

"I didn't steal it," Carrie squeaked. "I borrowed it, and no, I don't want to look at it, not anymore."

"Then put it back in the outgoing mail slot," Jo said. "No one will be the wiser."

"All of this excitement makes me want to throw up." Carrie clutched her stomach.

"It could have something to do with the three cinnamon rolls you ate earlier," Delta teased. "You do look a little pale. Maybe you should go inside and lie down."

"Yes. Yes, I think I will." Carrie let Delta lead her inside the house while Jo and Raylene waited in the driveway.

She joined her friends a short time later. "Poor thing. I think this is the most excitement she's had..."

"Since she claims she found Grasmeyer's wallet and someone ran her off the road the other night." Jo finished her sentence.

"True. Still, she rescued us from a sticky situation, so I think dropping off the mail she borrowed will even things out."

The women returned to the SUV and Jo climbed behind the wheel. She handed the envelope to Delta before buckling up.

Delta studied the front. "Now that's interesting. Check it out."

Chapter 13

"Check what out?" Jo shot her friend a sideways glance.

"It looks like some sort of legal correspondence." Delta tilted the envelope toward the light.

"We could steam it open," Jo joked.

"Joanna Pepperdine. That's as bad as stealing it in the first place."

"It was a joke."

"Lang and Brogan, Attorneys at Law, Kansas City."

"It's probably something from the divorce attorneys," Jo theorized. "The name sounds familiar. I think I've seen their billboards near Kansas City."

"I guess Laurie won't have to worry about that now." Delta set the envelope in her lap. "She'll be sitting pretty if you think about it...Grasmeyer's business, the house and I'm sure plenty of money. Laurie should be the prime suspect."

"She certainly had motive," Raylene said. "Maybe she set her husband up with a hefty life insurance policy and made sure she had an alibi before hiring a hitman."

"Don't forget about Wayne Malton. Grasmeyer tried to destroy his business." Jo grew quiet. She'd met Wayne a couple of times. He didn't strike her as a person who would kill another, but then again she didn't know him that well.

"Grasmeyer also filed complaints against Jesse McDougall. He's not the most pleasant person, either," Jo said.

"But that doesn't make him a killer." Raylene lifted her hands over her head. "I've been giving it some thought. I think it was a pre-meditated murder, not a murder of passion or rage."

Raylene explained her theory why it wasn't coincidental that Grasmeyer's jeep and body were found not far from the farm. "Think about it...most of the people in town were at the open house. What a perfect spot to plant a body."

"I think the killer planted his wallet, too. Someone who attended the open house murdered Grasmeyer." Jo stopped at the corner and then drove onto Main Street. "Let's start with the theory Carrie Ford is the killer. She murdered Grasmeyer, stole his wallet and planted it in my bathroom, pretending she found it. She left and then fabricated a story of how someone forced her off the road on her way home."

"What is her motive?" Delta asked.

"That's what's not adding up. As far as I can tell, Carrie has no motive."

"Pull up to the drop off bin." Delta pointed to the familiar blue drop box. When they reached the bin, she tossed the envelope inside.

"What if…" Jo started to pull away and then jammed on the brakes.

Delta flew forward. "Easy on the brakes."

"Sorry. I was thinking…what if Carrie did see someone inside the man's house the other night, as well as last night? What if during one of her nightly walks she saw Grasmeyer's killer and the killer spotted her?"

"Then the killer would want to get rid of Carrie, too," Raylene said.

"Precisely, and what better time and place than when she was leaving the open house," Jo said. "Nash just happened to be in the wrong place at the wrong time."

"Throw in a house full of former convicts and the list of suspects is endless."

The trio discussed the theory that someone plotted to kill Craig Grasmeyer. They waited until the evening before the open house, shot him and then dumped his body not far from the farm.

Carrie inadvertently caught a glimpse of the killer. The killer attended the open house and planted the wallet in the bathroom, knowing it would be found, and Grasmeyer's body discovered nearby. They saw an opportunity to take Carrie out, as well.

"It also could have been Laurie Grasmeyer." Jo pulled into the drive and parked off to the side.

Delta slid out of the SUV and wandered around front. "If the authorities are as close to making an arrest as Carrie claims, why would they bother searching the property?"

"Standard procedure," Raylene said. "The authorities would follow up on every lead, chase down every clue, which would include searching the victim's residence and questioning the spouse or in this case, the estranged spouse."

"Instead of clearing our name, we're still in the mix with a bunch of other people," Delta said.

"Misery loves company," Jo said.

"I better get going. I need to get ready for my shift." Raylene thanked them for letting her tag along and then headed to her apartment.

Jo cast an uneasy glance at Nash's workshop. "I'm getting a bad feeling about all of this. I think Nash is the number one suspect. He and Grasmeyer couldn't stand each other and Nash was the last person Grasmeyer called. He has no alibi, and Carrie claims Nash or someone driving a vehicle similar to our truck was the one who ran her off the road."

Jo consulted her watch. "I'm going to check on the gardens and clear my head. There's something nagging in the back of my mind. Maybe a brisk walk will clear the cobwebs."

She dropped her purse off before grabbing her garden boots. "C'mon, Duke. Let's head to the gardens." Jo waited for her pooch to join her, and the two tromped down the back steps.

Craig Grasmeyer's death troubled Jo more than she cared to admit. Someone - a killer - was targeting Jo, her residents and her employees.

What sort of evidence was the police hoping to find inside the Grasmeyer home? Had Carrie caught a glimpse of Grasmeyer's killer? If so and the killer knew it, Carrie's life might still be in danger.

Or maybe Carrie was wrong, and there was no one inside Grasmeyer's home.

What if Carrie was the killer? But why kill her neighbor? She quickly dismissed the thought. Carrie was an odd woman and conveniently in the wrong place at the wrong time, but she most definitely didn't fit a killer profile.

Still, Carrie knew Grasmeyer's gate combination and admitted she was familiar with Bugsy, Grasmeyer's cat.

The wife was the most obvious suspect, with Jesse McDougall a close second. He may have taken Grasmeyer out and planned to frame Jo or one of her residents. He would also know what type of vehicle Carrie drove.

She made a mental note to ask Delta if she remembered seeing Jesse McDougall at the open house. Maybe McDougall put his sister up to the dirty deed. Debbie Holcomb was at the open house.

Duke and Jo circled the smaller of the two gardens, inspecting the beets, carrots, cabbage and cauliflower, pleased with their progress and excited about the prospect of selling more produce with Nash's eye-catching wheelbarrow displays.

There were also several rows of sunflowers, one of Jo's favorite garden items. Jo's pup trotted up and down the rows, stopping occasionally to investigate.

Gary was the one who told Jo that Kansas was the Sunflower State, and that the beautiful blooms were a garden staple.

Since Gary's attack, he was a regular at the dinner table for Delta's Sunday evening feasts, and

Jo secretly suspected her employee had developed a soft spot for the widower, not that she would ever admit it.

It was something in the way Delta hovered over him, making sure he ate enough and then sending leftovers home. Jo teased her about it once, to which Delta vehemently denied any such level of interest.

Still, Jo swore there was a spark between them.

After finishing the first garden inspection, they wandered along the perimeter and property line, pausing when they reached the silo. Jo shifted her eyes and scanned the open fields remembering the sheriff's statement, how her property abutted the Indian reservation.

Was her property the location of a fierce tribal battle? She was beginning to wonder if perhaps maybe her farm was cursed. Jo dismissed the thought. God led her to the area and the home she had grown to love.

Not only was it home to her, but also to Delta, Nash and the women who counted on Jo to help them get back on their feet. No one, whether here in flesh and blood or spirit, could force them from their home.

Delta was buzzing around the kitchen when Jo returned. "I was thinking about what Carrie said, how the authorities were close to making an arrest and were there to search the Grasmeyer home. Do you think the killer will return to the scene of the crime?"

"We don't know if Grasmeyer was killed inside his home," Jo said. "What we do know is his body was found not far from here. It's a shame we don't know exactly where they found him."

"I know where they found his body." Delta wiped her hands on her apron. "My niece, Patti, told me it was right near the rear entrance to the Indian reservation's property. The reservation police helped the local authorities with the search. Nash knows exactly where it is. You can ask him to take you over there. I see the pickup pulling in the driveway now."

"Are you playing matchmaker again?"

"Maybe." Delta grinned. "Besides, you're his boss. You have a right to ride around with the hot hired help." She made googly eyes at Jo, who could feel a warm heat creep into her cheeks. "Stop."

"Ugh." Jo strode out of the kitchen.

Delta's laughter followed her out of the house.

Jo strode across the driveway. Of course, Nash was nice to Jo. She was his boss. He was nice to all of them. And yes, if she were completely honest with herself, Jo was attracted to him, but she chalked that up to spending years alone and on her own.

No, a man or even a flirty romance was not in the cards for Jo Pepperdine.

Nash had exited the truck; his back to her as he reached inside.

"Hey, Nash. I'm sorry to bother you."

Nash turned, a slow smile spreading across his face. "You're no bother, Jo. I've got all the time in the world for you."

"Yes...uh." Jo tripped over her words as she struggled to remember precisely why she was there. "I wanted to fill you in on our visit with Carrie who, by the way, is no longer certain our pickup truck forced her van off the road."

"That's a relief," Nash said. "I could use some good news."

"While we were talking about Craig Grasmeyer's death, I got to thinking about how one of us is the perfect person to take the fall for his death." She shared her thoughts on how the killer dumped Grasmeyer's body not far from the farm and his jeep just down the road. "We're the ideal suspects...all of us."

"I know, Jo. There's not much we can do. At least Carrie isn't claiming I'm responsible for her accident."

"Now she's claiming she saw someone inside Grasmeyer's house the other night while she was walking her cat."

"Carrie lives near Craig Grasmeyer?"

"Yep." Jo nodded. "They live in the same neighborhood."

"So maybe *she* saw the killer, and he or she tried to take Carrie out."

"I thought the same thing. Grasmeyer had his share of enemies, including his soon-to-be ex-wife, Jesse McDougall, the postmaster he filed complaints against, not to mention Wayne Malton, who was involved in some very public disputes with Grasmeyer."

"And me," Nash added quietly. "The man was a jerk and a shady businessman."

"Precisely." Jo clasped her hands. "I was thinking. Delta said the police at the Indian reservation helped locate Grasmeyer's body near the rear entrance to the reservation."

"Yep. I know where they found him."

"So...could we take a quick drive over there if it's not too much trouble?"

"Not at all." Nash held up a couple of shopping bags. "I'll drop this hardware inside, and we'll take a run over there."

"Thank you."

"You're welcome." Nash carried the bags inside before returning to the truck. "It's a beautiful day for a ride in the country. Have you ever visited the Indian reservation gift shops?"

"No. I've been meaning to stop by there. I hear they have some beautiful turquoise and silver jewelry."

"They do." Nash climbed behind the wheel. "I have a little extra time. If you're not in a hurry, after we have a look at the spot where they found Grasmeyer, we can run by the gift shops."

"That would be nice." Jo adjusted her seatbelt. "It is a gorgeous day. I walked the grounds and gardens. Did you know my property was an Indian battleground?"

"Yes, at least I heard the rumor. Don't know if I believe the spirits of the Indians haunt the place."

"But there are strange occurrences around Divine." Jo thought about Raylene's miraculous rescue, not to mention her own Divine intervention when she was nudged out of bed in the middle of the night, only to discover her bedroom wall was smoldering.

"God is our protector," Nash said.

"Yes, he is. I believe he brought me to Divine for a purpose...to help those women."

"And I'm grateful every day to have met you."

They both grew silent with Jo lost in her thoughts. God not only brought Jo to Divine, but he had also given her purpose in her life again. She thought back to the reason why she was here.

Jo had a unique connection to the women from the *Central State Women's Penitentiary*. Delta was the only one who knew Jo's secret. She also knew Joanna Pepperdine was an extremely wealthy woman.

In Jo's mind, her money was blood money...unearned and unwanted. For many years, it was a curse, until one day Jo stumbled upon an online flyer for a property auction - the McDougall property to be exact.

She gave it a quick glance before clicking away, but it was too late...the property haunted her, and she kept going back to it. As the date for the auction drew nearer, Jo drove out to the dilapidated farm to have a look around.

The moment she stepped out of the SUV, and her feet hit the ground, Jo knew she'd come home. From that moment on, she researched the area and the property. She'd contacted contractors along with an appraiser to get their opinions.

The night before the auction, Jo hadn't slept a wink. She wanted the property, needed the property. Finally, in the wee hours of the morning after Jo got up and ready, she hit her knees and prayed to God that if the farm was where He wanted her to be, He would help her purchase it.

The auction was packed. Many of the area residents were on hand, curious to find out what would happen to the farm. There were also several serious bidders, including out-of-town investors Jo suspected had their eye on the large chunk of land to develop.

They may have had deeper pockets than Jo, but none of them wanted it more than she did. One by one, they dropped out until it was just Jo.

She paid a little more than the appraisal's stated worth but it didn't matter. Joanna Pepperdine had finally found a place to call home and a purpose in life.

"We're here." Nash steered the truck off the side of the road and pointed to the sign, *Kansas Creek*

Indian Reservation. "I don't know the exact spot, but this is close."

Nash waited for Jo to join him near the bumper, and they began tromping through the thick brush. "Do you think there's a reason the killer chose this exact location?"

"Maybe," Nash shrugged. "I reckon they were looking for a road less traveled. This is the backside of the reservation, not the main road. Check this out." He knelt down. "It looks like two sets of tracks."

Jo studied the grass. Nash was right; it did look as if there were two sets of tracks in the tall grass. "You're right. So Grasmeyer may have had company - his killer." She slowly wandered along the side of the road. Grasmeyer may have been an awful man, but it was still a terrible way to die. She walked for several yards before turning around.

"Thank you for showing me the spot." Jo stepped around the front of the truck at the same time a thick cloud of dust billowed up, and a car careened around the corner.

Chapter 14

The vehicle came to an abrupt stop. A tall man, thin and with tanned skin emerged from the vehicle. "Can I help you?"

Nash moved protectively in front of Jo. "I'm Nash Greyson. This is Joanna Pepperdine. Joanna owns the former McDougall property over on D Road, *Second Chance Mercantile* and *Divine Baked Goods Shop*."

"I am Storm Runner, one of the security patrols for our reservation. I have heard of Ms. Pepperdine. You own the *Field of Blood*, the site of a fierce *Kansas Creek* battle. It is a cursed site."

"It may be a curse to the *Kansas Creek* people, but to me, it is a blessing." Jo changed the subject. "We're here because the authorities found the body of a Divine resident nearby."

"You're talking about Craig Grasmeyer. I met him once. He was not well-liked."

"He had his share of enemies," Nash agreed. "We heard someone from the reservation found his body."

"Yes. The local authorities were here to search the area after finding his abandoned vehicle. One of their men and one of our security staff found his body about twenty feet from the sign and near the back of your truck, in the ditch."

"You say you met Grasmeyer," Jo said.

"He and his wife visited the shops, and I remember because the man was rude to our people. I escorted him and his wife from the premises."

"I see." Jo tapped her chin thoughtfully. "So Grasmeyer and his wife visited the Indian reservation. "His wife...what did she look like?"

Storm Runner held a hand to his chest. "She was a small woman, only this tall and hair like fire."

"Red hair," Jo said.

"To match her spirit. She was not happy to be escorted off the premises."

"So she mouthed off to you," Jo said.

"Yes." Storm Runner grinned, displaying a dazzling set of pearly whites. "But I am accustomed to fiery women. My wife, Namid, she has a quick temper but her hair...it is not the color of fire." The man sobered. "The authorities have been to the reservation twice. We know little about the man's death, other than his body being found here."

"It's still under investigation," Nash said. "We planned to visit the reservation's gift shops after checking out the location."

"I will show you how to get there," Storm Runner said. "We will take the back way."

Despite the fierce expression on the Indian's face, Jo liked him. He seemed genuine. She was also fascinated with the tribal customs, and since they were neighbors, she decided it wouldn't hurt to get to know them better.

"Thank you, Storm Runner," Jo offered him a warm smile. "You must stop by the bakeshop the next time you're in the neighborhood and try some of our baked goods."

"I would like that. I will bring Namid." The man returned to his vehicle and motioned for them to follow him down the dirt road. He drove slowly, careful not to stir up more dust.

Nash draped his arm over the steering wheel, casting Jo a curious glance. "You like Storm Runner."

"Yes. He seems like a straight shooter, something I always appreciate. These people are our neighbors. I think it's in our best interest to stay on friendly terms with them."

"So they don't put a curse on you," Nash teased.

"God is bigger than any curse or Indian spirit." Jo wagged her finger in Nash's direction.

The path widened from a two-lane dirt road to a gravel road before they finally reached pavement. The reservation's shopping area was laid out in a wide arc with the buildings strategically placed in a semi-circle. While several of the structures shared common walls, there were also several detached buildings.

All of the buildings were constructed of the same worn and weathered wood. In the center was an Indian teepee.

They parked across from the teepee and Jo waited for Storm Runner to join them. "Is that an honest to goodness teepee?" She felt foolish as soon as the question was out of her mouth, but Storm Runner didn't make fun of her.

She could see he was proud of his home. "It is. Would you like to take a closer look?"

"I would love to." Jo clapped her hands.

Nash and she followed Storm Runner to the teepee's entrance. Circling the base of the teepee were bright red triangles. A stampede of wild horses galloped across the center, the backdrop a lighter shade of muted white.

The top of the teepee faded to black where several large, wooden poles extended skyward.

"The painted area around the bottom is what we call the bottom skirt. It symbolizes the earth's surface, and is a tribute to the importance of earth as the source of all physical life."

Storm Runner continued. "The top represents the upper limit of the physical world and symbolizes the sky. The center, and in this case the wild horses, are picture stories of human events. Sometimes they are birds, sometimes buffalos while others, fierce warriors fighting."

"Fascinating." Jo ran a light hand across the fabric. "The teepees must be made of some tough stuff to withstand the elements."

"Yes. All of them, including this ceremonial teepee, are custom-made."

Storm Runner explained the teepees were no longer made from animal skins. Instead, they consisted of woven cotton, made from organic fibers. "The outside is sealed with a special coating. They resist mold and mildew and are even flame retardant."

Storm Runner lifted the door flap, and Jo stuck her head inside. "Whenever possible the teepee entrance faces east, toward the rising sun."

"I see."

Near the entrance were several wicker baskets, brimming with thick furs. On the other side was a wooden platform. Clay pots, in an array of sizes and shapes, filled the platform. "What beautifully painted pots," Jo gushed.

"Our pots are all hand-painted and for sale in the store," Storm Runner pointed to a pile of charred sticks in the center of the teepee. "That is where we light the ceremonial fires." He lifted his hand. "The smoke drifts up and out the vented top."

"We no longer live in the teepees, but we still use them, and you will find them throughout the reservation. Some are plain, while others are ornate, depending on the owner and the story."

Jo and Nash stepped away from the teepee. "Thank you for explaining the significance. I can't wait to see what treasures I'll find inside the shops."

A man approached Storm Runner. "Chief Tallgrass is looking for you."

Storm Runner nodded. "I must go." He motioned to a road opposite the shopping area. "That road is the easiest way to exit the reservation."

Jo thanked him again for the history and tour before Nash and she headed inside the store.

Its size was impressive and reminded Jo of the mercantile and bakeshop where one store spilled into another.

There were intricate pieces of pottery, thick furs, blankets, decorative rugs and rows of dried herbs. Jo spent most of her time admiring the turquoise jewelry, which, according to the clerk, was handmade.

She almost purchased a turquoise necklace, but at the last minute, decided it wasn't practical and an impulse purchase. Instead, she chose a serving platter she hoped Delta would adore, along with a pot almost identical to the one she spied inside the teepee.

After paying for her purchases, Nash and she headed home. The drive to the main road was quicker than the drive onto the reservation.

Storm Runner was right...they had taken the long way. Not that Jo minded. It had given her a chance to check out the lay of the land.

Nash was quiet, and Jo gave him a shy glance. "Thank you for taking me to the reservation. I enjoyed it immensely."

"You're welcome. I think I enjoyed it just as much. The tribal people are good neighbors. We should make a point to support them more often."

"And tell our store customers about this place since it's off the beaten path." Jo made a mental note to tell the women about the Indian reservation when she chatted with them at dinner, and ask them to start mentioning it to the shoppers.

Back at the farm, Nash carried Jo's purchases to the house before returning to his workshop. She found Delta in the kitchen, a tantalizing aroma lingering in the air.

Jo's stomach grumbled. The cinnamon roll from earlier was long gone. "Something smells delicious. What are you making?"

"Cheddar biscuits. I whipped up a batch of my lip-smacking white chicken chili to go along with them."

Jo's mouth began to water as she peered into the enormous stainless steel pot, its contents bubbling away. "Do you need a taste tester?"

"You know me...I can always use a second opinion." Delta grabbed a bowl from the cupboard and ladled a large scoop into it. "You missed lunch. Did you check out the spot where Grasmeyer's body was found?"

"Thanks." Jo carried the bowl to the table. "Yes, and after we found it, we stopped by the Indian reservation to check out the gift shops." She grabbed a soup spoon and settled in at the table. "We met Storm Runner, one of their security officers."

Jo blew on the chili before taking a bite of the creamy garlic and chicken chili. "This is delicious. You make the best chicken chili this side of the Mississippi."

"Thanks. It turned out to be one of my best batches, if I do say so myself."

"I bought a serving platter and a pot. The platter is yours. I'm not sure what I'll do with the pot." Jo told her about the Indian teepee, the friendly people at the reservation, and then mentioned Craig Grasmeyer's visit to the reservation when he was escorted off the premises.

"Storm Runner was the one who escorted him and his wife off. He was being rude to the staff, and she was mouthing off. Storm Runner blamed it on her red hair."

Delta's eyebrow shot up. "Laurie Grasmeyer doesn't have red hair. Her hair is dark." She patted her hips. "Grasmeyer's wife is tall and a little on the plump side, kinda like me."

"Then he was there with another woman."

Jo inhaled the rest of the chili, leaned back in the chair and patted her stomach. "I can't wait for dinner."

Delta placed her hands on her hips. "Girl, I do not know where you put all that food. I sure wish I had the cute little shape you got. That's what caught Nash's eye."

"I have not caught Nash's eye. We're friends...or more like friendly employer/employee."

"Whatever." Delta waved dismissively. "So the Indians kicked Grasmeyer and his lady love off the property?"

"Yes, because he was rude to the employees." Jo picked up the serving platter. "Isn't this beautiful? It's hand painted."

"I love it." Delta took the platter from Jo and turned it over in her hand. "I'll wash it up and put some fruit on it for dinner."

"I'll clean it up while I wash my dirty bowl and silverware." Jo hand-washed her dishes and then offered to help in the kitchen, but Delta insisted she had everything under control.

Since Delta didn't need her help, Jo decided to catch up on some paperwork. When she reached her office, she turned her computer on and scanned the local news.

Splashed across the top of the page was a picture of a man and a caption underneath. *"Local businessman found dead. The authorities suspect foul play."* The story was time-stamped a couple of hours earlier.

She clicked on the article. The picture and caption were large, but the story was brief:

"Local businessman, Craig Grasmeyer's, body was found on the outskirts of Divine, Kansas, near the county line and the Kansas Creek Indian Reservation. Although the authorities haven't released the cause of death, an unnamed source claims he was shot multiple times."

Jo's stomach churned at the thought of discovering his bullet-riddled body. She continued reading:

"Devin Colette, our Divine local reporter, is on the scene in the small town after discovering the authorities have picked up a local resident for questioning."

Carrie was right. The authorities had been close to an arrest. When Jo read the next line, the room started to spin.

Chapter 15

"According to the same unnamed source, the authorities have detained Carrie Ford, a Divine resident and one of Craig Grasmeyer's neighbors."

"Delta. Come quick." Jo's chair toppled over as she scrambled to her feet. She ran into the kitchen. "Delta!"

"What?" Delta jumped. "Is the house on fire?"

"No. The *Smith County Herald* posted a story about Grasmeyer's death. He was shot multiple times."

"What an awful way to go."

"They picked Carrie up for questioning."

Delta's jaw dropped. "No way."

"Oh, yes. Come check it out."

Delta followed Jo to her office. She slipped her reading glasses on and read the story aloud. "Whoa, Bessie."

"Whoa, Carrie. What if Carrie is the killer?"

The pieces were beginning to fall into place...Carrie's claim she found Grasmeyer's wallet in Jo's guest bathroom, her insistence someone followed her from the open house and forced her van off the road. "Carrie set us up."

"Could be," Delta said. "Maybe she killed Grasmeyer and saw a perfect opportunity to frame you or even Nash. To cover up, she lied about someone forcing her off the road."

"She seemed very familiar with Grasmeyer's habits and the layout of his property."

"Not to mention she knew Grasmeyer's gate code," Delta said.

Jo snapped her fingers. "Red hair. Running Storm said Grasmeyer was with a woman with red hair. Carrie has kind of reddish hair. Maybe she and

Grasmeyer were having an affair. She killed him in a jealous rage."

"Carrie's hair isn't red. It's bottle-blond." Delta wrinkled her nose. "Besides, she doesn't strike me as Grasmeyer's type."

"What is Grasmeyer's type?"

"Good point." Delta dusted her hands. "Well, looks like the authorities have their man...er, woman." She headed back to the kitchen and Jo followed behind.

"The clues point to Carrie, but my gut tells me she was not responsible."

"I think your gut is wrong. The mystery has been solved," Delta said. "The authorities probably searched Grasmeyer's property, found some incriminating evidence and picked Carrie up."

"She saved our hides," Jo said. "If not for her, the authorities would have caught us snooping around Grasmeyer's property."

"But they didn't. Besides, we're not guilty…Carrie is."

Delta made some excellent points. Maybe Carrie and Grasmeyer were having an affair, and she killed him …or had some other reason to take Grasmeyer out. As Delta pointed out, she was familiar with the property layout, the interior layout, not to mention she knew his gate code.

Despite all of the evidence pointing to Carrie, Jo was convinced they were missing something.

During dinner, she picked at her food as visions of Carrie behind bars ran through her head.

"You're a million miles away, Joanna." Delta waved a hand in front of Jo's face. "Are you still stewing over Carrie?"

"Yes. I mean, the poor woman seemed terrified of jail time and now look at her. I doubt anyone even cares she's in jail."

"You don't know she's in jail." Delta dropped her chin in her hand. "I don't like the look on your face."

"What look?"

"You know what look...like you want to do something."

"I do. I want to talk to Carrie, but she's probably been arrested. The story sounded pretty cut and dried to me." Jo scooped up a spoonful of chili and watched it fall back into the bowl. "I wonder how prison food tastes."

"It's wonderful," Delta said. "Especially when I was the one making it."

"No offense. I forgot you're a former prison cook." Jo stared at the women seated around the table, her eyes resting on Raylene to her right. "What do you think, Raylene? You met Carrie. Do you think she's capable of committing murder?"

"I..." Raylene shook her head. "Honestly, she's a wildcard. I'm not sure she would be able to figure out how to shoot a gun, let alone trick the man into going with her to a deserted road and then fill him full of lead."

"See?" Jo said. "Raylene doesn't think she did it, either." She shoved her chair back and stood. "I'm sorry, but I can't sit idly by knowing an innocent woman might take the rap for a murder she didn't commit."

"What are you going to do?" Delta asked.

"I'm going to run down to the sheriff's station to see if they'll let me talk to her. Carrie needs a good lawyer by her side before they railroad her into a confession." Jo strode into the kitchen to grab the car keys.

Delta ran after her. "They aren't going to let you talk to her especially if she's being interrogated, and knowing how Carrie rambles; the interrogation could take several days."

"I have to try."

"Ugh." Delta clenched her fists. "Fine. I'll go with you."

"I'll go, too." Raylene stood in the doorway. "I have to agree with Delta. The investigators are not going to let you talk to Carrie. They may have already released her, and she's home."

"Then don't waste your time. I'll go by myself." Jo ran to her room to grab her purse. When she returned downstairs, Delta and Raylene were waiting by the door.

"You're going with me?"

"Against my better judgment," Delta said. "I think it's a waste of time. Even if the authorities coerce a confession, Carrie will likely retract it by morning."

Jo eased past Delta and headed out. Raylene followed behind, and Delta reluctantly brought up the rear. "I'm done fussing about it."

"Good, because I'm not going to change my mind. At the very least, someone needs to advise her to hire a decent lawyer." Jo waited until the women were inside the SUV before shifting into drive and pulling onto the road. "If my memory serves me, the sheriff's station is a couple miles out. I want to stop by Carrie's first. Raylene has a point. She may be home."

Jo drove straight to Carrie's place, turning onto Serenity Lane and easing into the woman's driveway. The place was dark and the lights off.

"I'll go knock." Raylene sprang from the vehicle and sprinted to the front door. She rang the bell and waited, before ringing it a second time.

Jo watched Raylene through the front windshield. "She's not home."

"Or not answering," Delta said.

"Her curtains are open. Why would she leave her curtains open and her lights off?"

Raylene stepped off the front porch before making her way to the side entrance. Moments later, she returned to the SUV and climbed in the back seat. "There's no one home. I heard Mr. Whipple."

"That means she's still at the sheriff's station." Jo shifted into reverse. "How do I get there?"

"Go back through town. Instead of turning right to head home, turn left at the stop sign. You can't miss it. They've got like fifty football field size lights out front."

They reached the station without incident. The interior of the station was flooded with bright white lights, similar to the ones illuminating the exterior. The interior's stark white walls matched the white tile floor and the white counter.

Raylene warily eyed the interior. "This place reminds me of somewhere else...except the walls are all gray and not white. I swore I would never step foot inside a police station again in my life, but here I am."

"Under completely different circumstances." Jo patted Raylene's arm. "You have nothing to fear."

The women made their way to the man standing behind the counter.

"Can I help you?"

"Yes, we're here to see if we can talk to someone who we believe is currently being questioned," Jo said. "Her name is Carrie Ford. Is she here?"

"I..." The man cleared his throat. "I can't answer that question."

Delta leaned an elbow on the counter, her gaze not wavering as their eyes met. "You just as much admitted it. So Carrie is here, she's being questioned and we're not allowed to talk to her."

The man folded his hands and started shaking his head.

"Is there anyone else we can talk to?" Jo asked in a soft voice. "Carrie is our friend, and we think she's being unfairly targeted."

The young man held up a finger. "Give me a minute." He hurried into the hallway, his quick steps echoing on the tile floor.

"You scared that poor desk clerk half to death," Jo scolded.

"He was scared before we ever got here," Delta said.

The man returned moments later. Following him was someone the trio knew well...it was Sheriff Bill Franklin. "Josh here said you want to have a word with Carrie Ford."

"Yes," Jo nodded. "We don't think she is responsible for Craig Grasmeyer's death."

The sheriff arched a brow. "Then who is responsible?"

"I...I don't know," Jo stammered. "It seems like Carrie couldn't possibly have murdered the man."

"Killers come in all shapes and sizes," the sheriff replied. "Besides, we haven't arrested Carrie. We're just questioning her."

"And her answers could change by tomorrow," Delta pointed out.

The sheriff held up his hands. "Listen, I appreciate how you want to help Carrie. There's nothing you can do at this point. We don't allow visitors, and she hasn't been charged with a crime."

"Yet," Raylene said.

The sheriff ignored Raylene's comment. "Why don't you ladies run along home and try not to worry about Carrie."

The conversation was over, and Jo knew there was zero chance the sheriff would let them talk to poor Carrie.

"Thank you for your time." Delta grabbed Jo's elbow and guided her out of the sheriff's station. She waited until all three of them reached the SUV. "See? This was a total waste of time."

"No." Jo stubbornly shook her head. "There's a reason the authorities picked Carrie up. Carrie told us earlier the investigators planned to search Grasmeyer's place." She began to pace. "Which means they must've found something when they were there earlier today."

"Or in Carrie's home," Raylene said. "What if they not only searched Grasmeyer's place, but also Carrie's place?"

"It's possible. It sure didn't take the authorities long to get their hands on a search warrant for my place," Jo said. "I have an idea."

Chapter 16

"Where are we going?" Delta peered out the window as they drove through downtown Divine.

"I want to swing by Carrie's place and maybe even Grasmeyer's home," Jo said.

"You want to break into Carrie and Grasmeyer's place?"

"No." Jo tightened her grip on the steering wheel. "We're not going to break into either one. First of all, there's a good chance Laurie Grasmeyer is staying at the house."

"True," Delta agreed. "And she'll call the cops in a heartbeat if she suspects someone is lurking around, especially after her husband's murder."

"Right. Plus, remember there's an electric gate."

"And Carrie knew the combination," Raylene reminded them. "Seriously, it's beginning to look as if dear Carrie isn't the victim she wanted everyone to believe."

When they reached the other end of town, Jo drove onto the dirt road and then into the paved neighborhood. Instead of turning onto Carrie's street, she turned onto the cul-de-sac leading to the Grasmeyer estate and slowed when they reached the front gate.

The gate was wide open, the driveway lights blazing brightly.

"It looks like an airport runway," Jo joked. "We can nix a quick look around this place."

"Unless we're keen on joining Carrie at the police station for questioning," Delta quipped.

"No thanks." Jo pressed on the gas, and they returned to the main road before turning onto Carrie's street for a second time.

Jo pulled into the drive and shifted into park. She swung the driver's door open.

"What are you doing?" Delta flung her arm across the seat to stop her.

"I'm going to do what any good friend or neighbor would do. I'm going to check on Mr. Whipple and make sure the place is locked. If Carrie is as forgetful as she seems, she could very well have left her doors unlocked."

Jo eased the door shut and tiptoed up the driveway making her way to the side porch and the breezeway. Delta and Raylene joined her.

"Mr. Whipple is in the breezeway," Raylene said. "I heard him earlier."

Jo reached for the doorknob, and Mr. Whipple let out a pitiful meow.

"The poor thing. He's probably wrapped around something in the breezeway." Visions of the cat with his leash tangled around his neck filled Jo's mind.

"We need to check on him." She cautiously eased the breezeway door open.

A dark shadow darted through the narrow opening and sprang off the steps. Raylene lunged forward in an attempt to grab the cat but Mr. Whipple was too fast, and he easily slipped past.

"Kitty!" Jo jumped off the steps and chased after the cat. She caught a glimpse of him as he streaked past the streetlight before he disappeared from sight.

"He's headed toward Grasmeyer's place!" Delta yelled. "We'll never catch him now."

"We have to try." Jo hustled to the end of the drive and along the sidewalk, all the while calling the cat's name. At one point, she heard a rustle in the bushes, but it was too dark to tell if it was him.

"C'mon, Mr. Whipple. You can't do this. Carrie will be heartbroken if you run off," Jo coaxed. She kept moving, keeping one eye on the sidewalk and the other on the low row of bushes.

She reached the end of the street. Mr. Whipple was nowhere in sight.

Delta, along with Raylene, raced after Jo and caught up with her at the corner. "You might as well forget about the cat. He's probably already over at Grasmeyer's place, and there's no way we can sneak onto the property."

"I can't leave the cat. Maybe if we knock on the door and explain what happened, Mrs. Grasmeyer will let us have a look around."

"Or maybe she'll call the cops," Raylene said.

"This is my fault. I let the cat out. I'll go it alone," Jo said bravely.

Delta pressed the palm of her hand to her forehead. "As much as I would like to do that, you know I can't. We're in this together. Just be ready to run, in case she chases us off her property."

The trio picked up the pace as they strolled along the driveway and approached the front porch. The porch's motion sensor light flooded the entrance.

Jo pressed the doorbell and took a step back, praying Laurie Grasmeyer wouldn't greet them with a gun. The door slowly opened and a tall, plump woman peered out. "Can I help you?"

"Yes. I..." Jo motioned to her friends. "We're friends of Carrie Ford, one of your neighbors, and were at her house checking on her cat. The cat darted out the door, and we followed him to your property. I was wondering if we could have a look around the yard."

"You're talking about that stinker, Mr. Whipple."

"Yes, Mr. Whipple. We heard he and your cat are friends," Delta said.

"It's a one-sided relationship if you ask me. Bugsy doesn't care too much for Mr. Whipple, but Mr. Whipple still comes around. Like owner like pet."

"I don't mean to show up on your doorstep, but I feel responsible for the cat getting loose and would be grateful if we could take a quick peek in the backyard," Jo said.

"I suppose so." The woman swung the door open and joined them on the porch. She eyed Jo curiously. "You look familiar. Do you live in the neighborhood?"

"No. I own *Divine Baked Goods Shop* and *Second Chance Mercantile*." Jo extended her hand. "Joanna Pepperdine."

"Ah. I've heard a lot about you. You certainly ruffled a few feathers around Divine after purchasing the McDougall place, especially old Jesse McDougall." The woman chuckled.

"He and his sister weren't too keen on me buying the place," Jo said.

"I think it looks great. Before I moved away a few weeks ago, I visited the mercantile and the bakeshop. You're doing a wonderful work there."

"Thank you." Jo's face warmed at the unexpected compliment. "I take it you didn't attend my open house the other night."

"Nope. I've been staying with family in Wichita while Craig stayed here at the house. I'm not one to air my dirty laundry, but I'm sure you heard we were in the midst of a messy divorce. I thought you were Vicki coming back again."

"Vicki?" Delta asked.

"Craig's office employee. She's badgering me to pay her, and I told her she would have to wait. I was getting ready to call the cops when I realized it wasn't her."

"Thank you for not doing that," Jo said. "I'm sorry to hear about your husband's death."

"My husband was no saint. I think the authorities are close to making an arrest. I thought for sure they were going after Wayne Malton."

Delta spoke. "Wayne Malton...the owner of the hardware store here in town?"

"Yep. Craig got a restraining order against him a couple of months back after he sold him some seconds on wood he was trying to pass off as premium grade. Wayne was so mad; he drove right over to the mill and confronted Craig."

"He could've ruined Wayne's business," Delta said.

"Yep. It got ugly. Anyhoo, like I said, Wayne threatened my husband, so he got a restraining order. Wayne is not the goody two shoes he wants people to believe."

"Why do you say that?" Jo asked.

"I have no proof, but I think Wayne knew Craig was selling him cheap seconds, hoping the lumber would pass for premium grade material to save a few bucks. He got caught and tried to shift the blame to my husband."

"Do you think Wayne murdered your husband?" Jo remembered that Wayne and his wife, Charlotte, were both at the open house.

"He's a nice enough guy, but you never know what someone will do when they get caught cheating." Laurie changed the subject. "I'll meet you around back to look for the cat. Mr. Whipple likes to hang out by the pool area. I noticed earlier that the door panel is out."

"He..." Delta pinched the back of Jo's arm, and she promptly closed her mouth. Perhaps it wasn't wise to confess they'd already visited the property.

Laurie promised to meet them around back while Delta, Raylene and Jo trudged around the side.

"Can you believe that about Grasmeyer?" Delta asked.

"He sounds...sounded like a snake," Jo said. "God rest his soul. I feel sorry for Laurie."

"She has a lot on her plate right now," Raylene said. "Sounds like the locals aren't particularly sympathetic toward her."

"Imagine that," Jo said grimly.

"But there are a lot of good people here, too," Delta argued. "Anywhere you go, you gotta take the good with the bad."

"You're right," Jo agreed. "I found that out the other night at the open house. There are some very nice people in Divine."

Laurie was waiting for them near the back screen door, the one with the missing panel, holding a docile Mr. Whipple. "Look who I found hiding behind the pots near the back of the pool."

"You naughty kitty," Jo took the cat from Laurie. "Thank you for rescuing Mr. Whipple, and I'm sorry we bothered you."

"I'm glad you bothered me," Laurie said. "It's been a long day...a long few months. The investigators are going to call me first thing in the morning to let me know whether they want to come back here and take another look around."

"Because they didn't find anything?" Raylene asked.

"Oh, they found some stuff all right, which is why I don't think they're going to charge anyone with Craig's murder, at least not yet."

Chapter 17

Laurie continued. "My husband was accumulating dossiers on several locals, learning their dirty little secrets. He had a whole file folder full of stuff on the Divine residents. Not only what I mentioned about Wayne Malton buying seconds, he was also digging into Jesse McDougall's habits. It appears that for years our fine postmaster was tossing marketing inserts in the dumpster behind the post office."

"Tossing out official US mail?" Delta's eyes widened.

"Yep. I have no idea how Craig found out unless he physically rummaged around inside the dumpster, which I wouldn't put past him. While we were still together, Craig was anxious for me to get a job at the post office. I think it was so I would be out of his hair so he could do his running around with some of the women here in town."

Jo shifted the wiggling cat to her other arm. "We better head back. Carrie will be frantic if she gets home and Mr. Whipple is missing." She thanked Laurie again for helping track down the cat and invited her to stop by the farm.

When they reached Carrie's place, she still hadn't returned.

Delta and Raylene waited outside while Jo inspected the inside of the breezeway. She checked Mr. Whipple's food and water dish before scratching his ears. "Carrie will be home soon. I'll check on you again in the morning, to make sure you're not alone."

The cat rubbed his head on Jo's hand and began purring. "Be a good kitty." She slowly backed out of the breezeway and pulled the door shut behind her.

Delta waited until Jo was inside the vehicle. "Did you see that?"

"See what?"

"A vehicle came creeping around the corner. They slowed when they got in front of Carrie's driveway. I tried to get a closer look, but by the time I turned around, they took off."

"Was it Carrie or the cops?"

"Nope." Delta shook her head. "It was a dark sedan."

Jo remembered Carrie mentioning that Mr. Whipple heard someone the other night. When Carrie got up to check, she noticed her exterior motion light was on, but there was no one there. "That's interesting." Jo reminded them of the conversation.

"You're right," Raylene said. "I remember her saying Mr. Whipple woke her up. Maybe she is being targeted."

"It could be she actually did see someone inside Grasmeyer's house the other night, after his death."

"Or it could be someone planned to stop by to visit Carrie and saw our vehicle parked in the driveway," Jo said.

"At this hour of the night?" Delta asked.

"True."

During the ride home, the trio discussed the possible suspects.

"The only suspect you haven't met is Vicki, Grasmeyer's employee," Raylene said.

"I wonder..." Jo began to formulate a plan. "What if we swing by Grasmeyer's lumberyard tomorrow morning under the guise of seeing if they have any lumber scraps to sell and then casually mention Grasmeyer's death?"

"I suppose it wouldn't hurt," Delta said. "The worst that could happen is she asks us to leave. We might as well stop by *Tool Time Hardware* while we're at it."

"Great minds think alike. I was going to suggest the same thing," Jo said. "Should we invite Nash to come with us?"

"I don't think he'll be keen on us snooping around in Grasmeyer's death."

"Good point. So we still have several suspects...Wayne Malton, the owner of *Tool Time Hardware* store. Wayne and Grasmeyer got into it, and Grasmeyer obtained a restraining order."

"Yep," Raylene said. "There's also Grasmeyer's employee, Vicki, who didn't report him missing until the police showed up and started asking questions."

"We also have Carrie and Jesse McDougall," Delta said. "Tampering with US mail is a federal offense. If Grasmeyer somehow managed to get his hands on proof the postmaster was throwing out mail, he could end up in prison."

"Last, but not least, we have Laurie Grasmeyer," Jo said. "She would have the most to gain from her husband's death. After breakfast tomorrow, we're coming back to town to shop for some lumber and check on Mr. Whipple."

*****

The morning couldn't come fast enough for Jo. She wavered between being convinced Carrie was responsible for Grasmeyer's death or possibly his employee, Vicki.

All of the evidence pointed to Carrie.

There was still Wayne Malton's restraining order, and the dirt Grasmeyer had on the postmaster. Perhaps it was a setup, and the wife was behind it all. It was possible Laurie made sure she had an ironclad alibi as to her whereabouts and then hired a hitman to take her husband out.

Jo hoped that once she met Vicki Talbot and stopped by Malton's hardware store, she would have a better idea if one of them might have been responsible for the man's death.

Delta, along with Raylene and Michelle, were already in the kitchen whipping up a pancake breakfast when Jo arrived. She helped set the table while the women assembled the food.

The others arrived promptly at seven. Breakfast was a lively affair, and Jo completely forgot they were hosting an end-of-the-summer blowout sale at the mercantile.

Some of the merchandise had been there since Jo opened the doors, and she was anxious to discount the goods to make room for new fall inventory.

Marlee told Jo that fall was a busy season in Divine. Tourists arrived in droves to visit the center of the country during the cooler weather. Divine also hosted its *Divine Fall Festival,* an annual event. It included scavenger hunts, trick or treating for the tots, a baking contest and a parade.

In anticipation of the busy season and upcoming festival, Jo spent the previous week sorting through the inventory figuring out what she wanted to put on clearance.

Sherry, one of the residents, loved tinkering around on the internet and found a site to list the sale items.

Between that and Jo's idea to add a clearance flyer to the town's bulletin boards, she hoped to rake in a tidy sum from the sale.

With some retail history under her belt, Jo had a better idea of what would sell and what would sit on the shelves collecting dust. Children's clothing was always a hot seller, along with small appliances, designer clothing, collectible cookware and video games.

Shoppers were always asking about old or antique books, something Jo had never considered sourcing but added to her growing list.

There was also quality furniture, or as Sherry informed her, the "shabby chic" look was still hot, as well as craftsmen items. Nash's handcrafted woodworking items were always popular.

Jo poured a generous amount of syrup on top of her small stack of pancakes and passed the bottle to Michelle. "I planned to run into Divine to take care of some errands this morning, but if you need me for the sale, I can do it tomorrow."

Leah, the resident Jo put in charge of the sale, shook her head. "I think we can handle it." She turned to Kelli, one of the other residents. "Don't you think?"

"We've got it covered. Besides, Nash will be around to help out in a pinch."

"I'll hang around for as long as you need me," Nash said.

"We'll always need you," Kelli flirted.

"I hope so." Nash caught Jo's eye at the other end of the table, and he winked.

"Yes. Of course we need you." Jo lowered her gaze and furiously sawed away at her pile of pancakes.

Delta kicked her under the table, and Jo shot her a hard look.

Her friend smiled innocently. "We ran into Laurie Grasmeyer last night. She has a whole list of people she thinks may have been responsible for her husband's death including Wayne Malton."

"Wayne wasn't a fan of Grasmeyer's," Nash said. "It may take the investigators months to finish interviewing everyone."

Breakfast cleanup was quick and after they finished, the women headed back to their apartments to get ready for the day. Raylene was the last to leave. "I'm sorry I can't go with you this time."

"Do you have any sleuthing advice?" Delta asked.

"I think you two can handle it. All of the suspects, other than Carrie, have a motive, and most had the opportunity." Raylene absentmindedly tapped her foot on the linoleum floor. "I keep thinking somehow there's a link to this place. The timing of

Grasmeyer's death wasn't coincidental, nor was the place where his body and vehicle were found."

"Which is why I'm leaning toward Carrie," Delta said. "Although we still don't have a motive."

"Right..." Raylene shrugged. "I'll give it some thought. Maybe by the time you come back, you'll have more information, and I can help you start piecing the clues together."

Delta and Jo left right after breakfast. Their first stop was Grasmeyer's lumberyard, a drab industrial metal pole building on the outskirts of town.

The gravel parking lot was filled with ruts and in need of attention. Front and center was a service door and over the door a rusted metal sign, *Grasmeyer Wholesale Lumberyard. Walk-ins Welcome.*

"This is it?" Jo wrinkled her nose.

"Not much to look at." Delta exited the SUV and joined Jo near the entrance. The door was locked. She rapped lightly, but no one answered.

Jo bounced on her tiptoes and peered into the grimy window. "I don't see anyone around."

"Me, either."

The women started to walk away when the door creaked open. "Can I help you?"

Jo turned back and found a dark-haired woman with wire-rimmed glasses standing in the doorway. "Yes, I'm Jo Pepperdine. I was wondering if you had any scrap lumber for sale."

The woman eyed Jo's expensive SUV. "You're gonna load lumber in that?"

"I'm only looking for a few scraps, if you have them."

The door opened wider. "Hey...I know you. You're the crazy lady who bought the old McDougall place and is harboring hardened criminals."

"I am not harboring anyone."

"Whatever. We're closed." The woman started to slam the door in Jo's face, but she was too fast and wedged her shoe in the gap. "Vicki, right?"

The woman kicked at Jo's foot. "Get your foot out of the doorway, or I'll call the cops."

"You could help solve your boss' murder," Jo blurted out.

"If you really want to know what happened to Craig, go talk to Carrie Ford instead of bothering me. I told the cops the same thing."

"Why Carrie?"

Instead of replying, the woman shoved Jo's foot out of the way and slammed the door in their faces.

"What an unhappy woman," Delta said. "And a waste of time. Let's get out of here before she makes good on her threat."

The women returned to the vehicle and climbed inside. "Carrie...that's it." Jo snapped her fingers. "Delta. Carrie was seeing Grasmeyer. Laurie hinted at it the other night when she said her husband was trying to get her a job at the post office so he could do his running around. He was cheating on his wife. That's why Carrie knew his gate code, why she was familiar with the layout of his house not to mention the property. Grasmeyer and Carrie were having a fling."

"Jo, I think you may be onto something," Delta said. "No wonder the cops picked Carrie up. I guess there's no need to stop at the hardware store. The authorities already have Grasmeyer's killer. I always suspected it was her."

"Maybe. I'm still not convinced." Jo glanced at the clock. "Since we're already in town, I would like to stop by there. I need to find something for Gary to rig up in the gardens to keep the deer out."

Jo drove back to Main Street. She eased the vehicle into an empty parking spot in front of the hardware store and shifted into park. "You don't have to go in."

"And miss out on all of the excitement of shopping at a hardware store?" Delta joked.

"Very funny." Jo followed Delta inside. The women wandered up and down the aisles until Jo found a roll of mesh wire on clearance. "I wonder if this would work."

"It's worth a try." Delta grabbed hold of the corner. "It seems pretty sturdy."

"And the price is right." Jo carried the wire to the checkout. Wayne was behind the counter, ringing up a customer's purchases.

She waited until the customer left, and then handed him the wire.

"Looks like you're gearing up for another project."

"The projects are never-ending. We're having trouble keeping the deer and critters from eating our fruits and vegetables. I thought maybe Gary could rig something up to keep them out."

"This might work. I also have some natural repellent. It's one hundred percent organic so it won't hurt the food."

Wayne led the women to the gardening section where he showed them a pallet loaded with large bags. "This stuff works double-duty. Not only will it help keep the weeds out, but it will also keep the pesky varmints away."

Jo studied the bag on top. "I'll take one of these and the wire. Maybe we can try the granules in one garden and the fencing in the other to see which works better."

Wayne lifted the bag, and the women followed him to the checkout.

"Thank you for coming to the open house. I enjoyed meeting your wife, Charlotte," Jo said.

"Thank you for hosting it. Maybe one of these days, we'll have you all over for dinner...you, Nash, Gary and Delta."

"I would like that. Do you live close by?"

"Yep." Wayne pointed to the ceiling. "Charlotte and I live upstairs."

"How convenient." Jo grinned. "I guess you can't make excuses for not going to work."

Wayne chuckled. "The boss can't make excuses." He sobered. "I was sorry to hear about Craig Grasmeyer's death, although I wasn't a fan."

Jo wasn't sure how much she should admit to knowing about Wayne's dislike of the man and merely nodded.

"Heard the authorities picked up Carrie Ford for questioning last night." Wayne finished ringing up Jo's purchases and handed her the receipt. "For the life of me, I'll never figure out what the women in this town ever saw in Grasmeyer."

"You knew Grasmeyer was seeing Carrie?" Delta asked.

"Among others," Wayne said. "My guess is Laurie got fed up with his shenanigans and finally left."

"I never met him," Jo said.

"He wasn't a good man. If he could figure out a way to cheat you, he would do it in a heartbeat. Heck, he probably swindled his own mother. I'll carry the stuff to your car."

Wayne grabbed the bag of repellant and wire and followed Jo and Delta to the SUV. She opened the back and watched him set it inside.

"Jesse McDougall was in here this morning. It appears the authorities are questioning him, too."

"We heard, something about destroying the mail or improperly disposing of it," Delta said.

"Yep. Guess Grasmeyer had a whole file he was keeping on the postmaster's activities. He had photos of mail dumped in the bins out back, including dates and times. You name it." Wayne closed the back of the SUV. "All thanks to his dear sister, Debbie."

"But why would Holcomb tell Grasmeyer her brother was disposing of the mail?"

"Grasmeyer and Debbie Holcomb were an item," Wayne said.

"I thought...he and Carrie were an item."

"And Debbie. Grasmeyer was making his rounds, wherever he thought it might benefit him. My theory is he was using Holcomb to get dirt on her brother, Jesse."

"That's crazy," Jo said. "Why would Debbie Holcomb throw her own flesh and blood under the bus?"

"There's no love lost between them. It all started with your place. Those McDougalls fought like cats and dogs, which is another reason they lost the place. They were suing the pants off each other."

Jo thanked Wayne for carrying her purchases to the SUV and then watched him make his way back inside the hardware store. "That was an enlightening conversation."

"Yep," Delta agreed. "There are so many persons of interest in Grasmeyer's death; the police must have their hands full trying to figure out who took the man out."

"Let's head home." Jo motioned to Delta. "Wayne gave me an idea. I have a new project I want to run by you."

Chapter 18

"Remind me again, why you wanted to come up to this creepy old attic?" Delta hovered near the bottom of the narrow stairs leading to the third floor.

"Because I want your opinion. I'm thinking about tackling a new reno project."

"As if you don't already have enough projects to work on around here."

"But this is wasted space." Jo climbed to the top and stepped into the cavernous room.

A lingering stale smell filled the air. Small beams of light filtered through the louvered gable vent leading to the outdoors.

"This place gives me the heebie-jeebies," Delta joined her. "If ever a place was haunted, this is it."

"In its current condition, I can't say as I disagree with you." Jo walked to the center of the room and spun in a slow circle. "Just look around. This attic has a lot of potential."

"Potentially haunted."

"Very funny. I mean potential as a fixer-upper." Jo quickly warmed to the idea. "With a few sheets of drywall, some new oak floors and a couple of coats of paint, this would make a cozy little book nook."

Delta curled her fingers and crept toward Jo. "Perfect for reading evening ghost stories."

"Stop it." Jo swatted at her friend. "I'm serious."

"Well, you can have it. You can turn this place into the Taj Mahal, and I won't come up here to visit." Delta wandered past Jo and made her way to the rafters. "There's something over here."

"Where?" Jo crossed the room.

Delta cautiously ran her hand along the top of the joist. She pulled out a small brown box and handed it to her friend. "Looks like this has been here for a while." She pulled out a second box.

A puff of dust filtered through the air. Delta covered her nose. "Achoo!"

"God bless you. Let's see what we've got." Jo took the other box and set them both on the attic floor. She flipped the flaps on the larger one and pulled out a stack of yellowed letters, tied together with a purple ribbon. She set them off to the side and grabbed a stack of postcards, her eyes narrowing as she studied the date.

October, 1920. Dear Aunt Myrtle. We are readying for the winter season and hope you and Uncle Frank will have another mild winter. With love, Henry and me. The postcard was signed Anna McDougall.

"This box belongs to the McDougall family." Jo placed an empty perfume bottle on top of the greeting cards and reached inside the box again. "Aha." She picked up an antique picture frame of three unsmiling people. "Do these look like

McDougalls to you?" She turned the frame so Delta could see.

"Yeah. They all have the same unhappy expressions."

"This stuff has to be theirs." Jo ran a light hand across the frame before carefully setting it back inside the box. "I should return these boxes to the family."

"I'm sure they'll want them, especially if there's anything of monetary value," Delta said.

Jo placed the items back inside the boxes and carried them down the steps. Delta ran after her, slowing just long enough to shut the light off. "Have you tried calling Carrie yet?"

"No. I need to check on her." Jo left the boxes on the table near the front door and made a beeline for her office. She grabbed her cell phone and dialed Carrie's number.

"Hello?"

"Hi, Carrie. It's me, Jo."

"Hello, Jo."

"I wanted to let you know that Delta and I stopped by your place last night to check on Mr. Whipple."

"You let him out."

"He snuck by me, but we found him over by Grasmeyer's place. I took him back home and left him in the breezeway after I made sure he had food and water."

"He's gone." Carrie's voice cracked. "I tried looking for him over at Grasmeyer's place, but he's not there."

"I...I'm certain that Mr. Whipple was in the breezeway when I left last night. I even checked to make sure the door was shut."

"Then someone else let him out. More than likely the same person who is after me. The police think I killed Craig." Carrie started to cry.

"Oh, dear." Jo gave Delta a helpless look as she pointed at the phone. "Would you like me to come over and help you search for him...your cat, I mean?"

"It's no use," Carrie whispered. "My only friend is gone."

"Carrie...we can find Mr. Whipple. I'll be there in a little while. Hang on...I'll be there as soon as I run a quick errand in town." Jo didn't give Carrie time to answer before disconnecting the call. "Someone let Mr. Whipple out last night after we left."

Delta rubbed her brow. "Remember when I said I saw someone drive by real slow while you were checking on the cat?"

"You're right. Carrie said someone was after her. I was thinking about the boxes we found in the attic. I can kill two birds with one stone and drop them off at the post office on my way to Carrie's place."

"I'll go with you," Delta said. "I feel somewhat responsible for Carrie's cat, too."

"You drive, I'll ride." Jo grabbed the boxes while Delta went to get her purse and the keys.

They climbed into the SUV and Jo set the boxes on the floor. "Maybe by the time we reach Carrie's place, Mr. Whipple will have already found his way back home."

"If he's not at the Grasmeyer place, I don't know where he could be." Delta stopped at the end of the drive. She looked both ways before pulling onto the road.

"Do you think I'm on the right track in helping the women?"

Delta shot Jo a puzzled look. "Now where did that come from?"

"I dunno," Jo shrugged. "The other day, during the ride to *New Beginnings*, Raylene showed me a paper with the list of their house rules and one of them included having to find a job."

"But the women do have jobs, here at the farm."

"Right, but even so…" Jo's voice trailed off as she stared out the window.

"You don't think you're completely preparing them for the outside world," Delta guessed.

"Exactly. I want to protect them, to give them a fighting chance but I wonder if by not allowing them to work outside the farm I'm insulating them too much, that I'm being over-protective."

"You're their mentor - not their mother. The women are all adults," Delta said. "I can tell you one thing for certain…not a single one of those women is in a hurry to leave."

"Which is another concern. The goal is to help them develop the skills to make it on their own, so they can eventually leave the farm and we can continue to bring in others who need a second chance."

"I hadn't thought of it. You could be right." Delta tapped the steering wheel. "What if you put the word out to Marlee at the deli and maybe even

Claire who owns the antique store and laundromat that the women might be in the market for part-time jobs?"

"That's a great idea," Jo said. "Do you think it's something they might be interested in entertaining?"

"Why not? Marlee was telling me just the other day that she needed to start looking for a part-time server to work through the fall at least until after the fall festival."

Delta and Jo discussed the possibility of the women finding jobs outside the farm while continuing to work there, as well.

"I think we should start with Sherry," Jo said. "At least offer her the opportunity first, since she's been with us the longest."

"We'll run it by Marlee next time we see her." Delta and Jo's first stop was the post office. Delta waited in the SUV while Jo carried the boxes inside. She returned moments later, boxes still in hand.

"You didn't leave them with Jesse McDougall?"

Jo climbed in and set the boxes in her lap. "You're not gonna believe this."

Chapter 19

"Jesse McDougall wasn't there. The woman behind the counter couldn't tell me when he would be back."

"Huh. Maybe he's been placed on leave because of the investigation."

"That's what I think. Let's drop the boxes off at Debbie Holcomb's place."

"Are you crazy? The last time we were there, she ran us off her property."

"I know. I remember, but I was thinking about how she must feel, how a complete stranger blew into town and snatched the family homestead out from under her nose. I might be angry, too," Jo said. "I'm going to apologize to Debbie and this is going to be my peace offering to try to make amends. This town is too small to have enemies."

"Fine, but don't say I didn't warn you." Delta drove to Debbie's place and stopped near the front curb.

"You're not pulling in the drive?"

"No. I figure it's safer to park out here. That way we can make a quick getaway if she comes after us."

Jo reached for the door handle. "Wish me luck."

"Good luck. You're gonna need it."

Jo climbed out of the vehicle and hurried to the front of the house. She stepped onto the stoop and rang the doorbell.

Yowl. There was an odd noise echoing from inside, but no one answered.

Jo tried again but there was still no answer. She leaned to the side and peered into the living room window. A yellow flash zipped by and then Jo heard the noise again.

She stepped off the stoop and made her way to the side door. She shaded her eyes and peered through the glass pane. The garage was empty. Jo twisted the knob but the door was locked.

She retraced her steps and set the boxes in front of the door and under the covered awning before returning to the SUV.

Delta waited until Jo opened the passenger door. "She wasn't home?"

"Nope. I need a pen and piece of paper." Jo rummaged around in her purse until she found an old grocery list and an ink pen. She scribbled a quick note, telling Debbie that she found the boxes in the attic and thought they might belong to the family.

Jo strode back to the porch where she tucked the note inside the box on top and then returned to the vehicle. "Hopefully, she'll notice the boxes on the front stoop. It doesn't look like rain, and they're protected by the awning."

"That's very nice of you, Jo, to return the family's belongings, I mean."

"Thanks, Delta. I would hope if it was me, someone would do the same." Jo dusted her hands. "Well, we have our first good deed for the day under our belts. Now let's head over to Carrie's place to see if we can track down her cat."

It was a short drive from Debbie Holcomb's house to Carrie's place, less than a mile. Delta turned onto her street and slowed when they got close. She pointed to the sedan parked in Carrie's driveway. "It looks like she has company."

"Maybe she's assembled an entire search party," Jo joked.

Delta parked on the side of the street and the women began walking single file past the vehicle.

"Look." Delta swung her arm out, almost clotheslining Jo. She pointed to the front of the vehicle and the crumpled bumper.

"Looks like someone was involved in a fender bender."

"Or maybe they forced someone's vehicle off the road. I recognize this car. It's the same one that almost ran us over in their driveway the day we were delivering baked goods for Marlee."

Jo's heart skipped a beat. "You're right. This is Holcomb's car. I'm getting a bad feeling."

Chapter 20

Jo's scalp began to tingle. "I saw something inside Holcomb's living room when I peeked in the window. What if Holcomb is the one who took Carrie's cat?"

"Let's not freak out. We need to stay calm. We'll sneak around the side and try to have a look in the window to see what's going on."

"Right," Jo swallowed nervously and nodded.

The women eased past Holcomb's sedan, creeping forward until they reached the side of the house.

Jo gripped the edge of the windowsill, slowly lifting her head in an attempt to see inside the mudroom window.

"Do you see anything?" Delta whispered.

"No."

The women inched along the walkway until they reached the back and what Jo remembered was the kitchen window. She slid behind a rosebush and slowly lifted her head.

"Uh." Jo dropped down. "I spotted Holcomb. She's standing at the kitchen table. I can't see anything else."

Delta and Jo traded places.

Delta slowly inched upward, keeping close to the edge of the window frame. "Umpf." She ducked back down. "She has a gun."

"Who has a gun?" Jo asked.

"Holcomb. She's holding a gun. We have to call the police."

Jo dropped to her hands and knees. She crawled across the backyard until she reached a row of potted flowering plants. Delta crawled in behind her.

"I can't believe this." Jo's hand shook as she pulled her cell phone from her pocket and dialed 911.

"911. What is your emergency?"

"This is Joanna Pepperdine. I'm at 121 Serenity Lane in Divine. I believe there's a possible hostage situation or a dangerous situation inside the home involving the resident."

"121 Serenity Lane."

"Yes. We believe one of the occupants is armed."

"I'm dispatching a patrol car now."

Jo thanked the 911 operator and slid the phone back in her pocket. "What if I spotted Mr. Whipple inside Debbie's house?" Jo whispered. "We need to make our way back to the front to meet the police."

The women crept along the perimeter of the property and returned to the SUV, just in time to flag down a patrol car that turned onto Carrie's street.

Jo waited until the officer exited his patrol car. "We believe Carrie Ford, the owner of this home, may be in danger. The vehicle in the driveway belongs to Debbie Holcomb. She's inside and she has a gun."

The officer nodded toward Carrie's house. "Did you see a gun?"

"I'm almost positive I did," Delta said.

The officer reached for his radio. "This is Officer Denco. I need backup at 121 Serenity Lane in Divine."

Moments later, two more patrol cars arrived, blocking off the street.

Officer Denco and the other officers fanned out, stealthily making their way toward Carrie's home.

"Please, God, protect Carrie." A wave of terror washed over Jo as she watched the officers surround the property.

The officers sprang into action as two of them barged through the side door.

Jo braced herself for the sound of gunfire, but there wasn't any. It seemed like an eternity before the officers emerged. Two of them escorted a handcuffed Debbie Holcomb to the back of one of the patrol cars and placed her inside.

Carrie appeared moments later, her face pinched and pale and clutching an officer's arm.

"Let's go." Jo grabbed Delta's arm and they ran to Carrie's side. "Are you okay?"

"She was going to kill me." Carrie's voice trembled. "She forced me to write a suicide note. Mr. Whipple is still missing."

"No." Jo thought about the delivery to Holcomb's house, how she heard a noise and saw something yellow dart across the room. "I'm not positive but Mr. Whipple may be safe. He may be inside Debbie's house."

"You saw him?" Carrie gave Jo a hopeful look.

"Maybe. Please don't get your hopes up." Jo quickly changed the subject. "I think Debbie is the one who forced your van off the road."

"The police told me you called 911 when you noticed Debbie's car parked in my driveway. She called me this morning and said she found Mr. Whipple and was going to bring him home." Carrie explained that when Holcomb arrived, she told her she kidnapped Mr. Whipple. "She pulled out a gun and forced me to write a suicide note."

"She forced you into confessing that you killed Craig Grasmeyer," Jo guessed.

"Yes and that I used his gun to kill him, the same one she was holding. That's why I committed suicide...because I couldn't live with myself."

Sudden goosebumps covered Jo's arms. "Holcomb killed Grasmeyer using his own gun. She was going to kill you with that same gun."

Carrie pressed her trembling hands to her cheeks. "Now I know why she was wearing gloves. I would be found holding the weapon that killed both Craig and me."

"Debbie Holcomb almost got away with the perfect murders."

Chapter 21

Jo breezed into the kitchen. "I spoke with Sheriff Franklin. Carrie was right...Debbie Holcomb was using Grasmeyer's gun. They found Mr. Whipple in Holcomb's house, and they also found something else."

"His missing watch," Delta guessed.

"Yep. Looking back, I think Debbie saw the open house as a perfect setup to make us the potential suspects and to take Carrie out. When that didn't work, she kidnapped the cat, forced Carrie to write a suicide note and then planned to kill her."

"I was thinkin' about this earlier," Delta said. "Remember when Marlee told us Grasmeyer claimed his wife, while they were still together, was a shoe-in for the job as postmaster?"

"Yeah."

"That's because Debbie Holcomb told him her brother was disposing of the mail in the dumpster. Grasmeyer was using Debbie, the same way he cheated and used everyone around him. She must have figured out what he was doing and confronted him. They fought, and she killed him in a fit of rage."

Delta opened the oven door and placed the tins of chocolate chip banana nut muffins in the oven. "I invited Carrie over for coffee. Ever since she found out Craig Grasmeyer was running around with Debbie, she's been depressed. She feels duped by the man."

"Along with several other locals," Jo said. "I feel a little guilty for thinking Carrie was responsible for his murder."

The front doorbell chimed, and Jo hurried to open it. Carrie stood on the other side. "I hope I'm not too early. I couldn't remember exactly what time Delta told me to be here."

"You're fine." Jo motioned her inside and led the way into the kitchen. "She just put a batch of her delicious chocolate chip banana nut muffins in the oven."

Delta was already pouring the coffee when Carrie and Jo joined her. She carried the cups to the table and handed one to each of them.

"Thank you, and thank you for saving my life. The police found my cat inside Debbie's house."

"That's what Sheriff Franklin said." Jo shot her friend a triumphant look. "See? Our good deed was worth the effort."

"I guess I was wrong again." Delta rolled her eyes. "And now that you helped crack the case you think you're the next Jessica Fletcher."

"I feel like such a fool," Carrie said. "Craig wasn't a good man. I can see that now. We started seeing each other after Laurie left, and I always wondered why he insisted on keeping our relationship a secret.

It's my fault for getting involved with a still married man in the first place. I'm such a dingbat."

"No, you're not." Jo smiled gently. "We all make mistakes. It doesn't make you stupid. It makes you human."

Carrie's sad expression was replaced by an angry look. "I hope the judge throws the book at Debbie Holcomb. She tried to kill me...twice."

"She's a troubled woman," Jo said. "Her brother, Jesse, is also in a precarious position. The authorities are investigating him for mail tampering."

The kitchen timer chimcd. "The muffins are ready." Delta pulled the muffins from the oven while Jo refilled their coffee cups.

While they ate, the women discussed the upcoming fall season and Divine's fall festival. "I'm thinking of entering my cinnamon spice sugar cookies in the baking contest. Someone needs to give Marlee a run for her money," Carrie said.

"A baking contest?" Jo eyed Delta over the rim of her coffee cup. "Are you entering the baking contest?"

"I...maybe." Delta wiped an imaginary crumb off the table. "I didn't last year."

"You should enter your cookies and cream raspberry dream bars," Carrie said. "Those dream bars will definitely give Marlee a run for her money."

"I take it Marlee has won the contest before," Jo said.

"Every year," Carrie and Delta said in unison.

"For the past five years," Delta added.

Carrie polished off her muffin and downed the last of her coffee. "I better get going. I want to stop by Claire's antique shop on my way home."

Delta and Jo carried the coffee cups to the sink and then accompanied Carrie to her van where she showed them the damage to her rear quarter panel.

"I decided to file a claim after all. The insurance company is insisting I take a driver's fitness test."

"Really?" Jo asked. "They're questioning your driving abilities?" Carrie was a little scatterbrained at times, but she seemed capable of operating a motor vehicle.

"I guess if you've had more than two accidents in a year, they want you to take a driving test before renewing your policy or processing a claim."

Jo inspected the damage. "How many accidents have you had?"

Carrie climbed in and rolled the window down. "Let me think…if you don't count the time I forgot to remove the gas nozzle at the gas station before driving off, there have only been three, including being forced off the road."

"Four?" Jo gasped. No wonder the insurance company was questioning Carrie's driving abilities.

"I wasn't ticketed for any of them. I was thinking, if you had some free time next week, it might be fun for us to hang out together."

The look on Carrie's face was hopeful, and Jo didn't have the heart to tell her 'no.'

"What do you have in mind?"

"I can teach you about taxidermy. I'm getting ready to work on a piece for my neighbor, Vivian. She lost her parrot, Bartholomew. He keeled over in his cage a couple of days ago. Vivian wants me to help make Bart her 'forever pet.'"

"Forever pet?"

"Taxidermy. She wants me to stuff him. We're kind of running out of time, though. Maybe I'll get started on Bart, and we can work on another project."

"That sounds..."

"Gross," Delta offered.

"Oh, it's loads of fun. How does next Tuesday sound?"

"I..." Jo and Delta exchanged a frantic glance.

"Perfect," Carrie beamed. "Mornings work best for me. Say around nine?"

"Nine it is," Jo said helplessly. "See you then."

Carrie was still smiling as she gave them a jaunty wave and drove off. She got to the end of the drive, paused briefly and then peeled out.

"I don't know what to think."

"Carrie is a one of a kind, I'll give you that," Delta shook her head. "Maybe she'll forget all about stuffing family pets, and we'll be off the hook."

"Somehow I don't think so. I just don't think so."

Delta flung her arm around Jo's shoulders. "Tomorrow is our big day."

"Right. I almost forgot. Our new resident is arriving." Pastor Murphy had been busy. When he found out about a recent resident's unexpected departure, he told Jo there was another inmate ready to be released whom he thought might be a perfect fit.

Jo told him to go ahead and send the woman's information. After poring over Tara's file and completing her due diligence of background checks and prison records, Jo deemed her a potentially good fit.

Jo had decided she wanted to meet the woman prior to her release and accompanied Pastor Murphy to the prison to chat with her.

Her story was so much like the others...she'd had a troubled childhood, gotten in with the wrong crowd and began using drugs. Tara's record included several arrests for prostitution to support her drug habit.

Drugs took over Tara's life, and she found herself involved in an armed robbery, along with her boyfriend. Convicted for her part, the woman spent several years in prison and was scheduled for a release.

Pastor Murphy was a regular visitor at the women's prison, talking to those who needed counseling as well as those close to release, which is how he found out about Tara.

"You haven't said too much about Tara," Delta said. "What do you think?"

"I...think she'll be a good fit. She seems determined to start over. She swears she's had no contact with her druggie ex-boyfriend, her accomplice in the armed robbery. Tara has a daughter who lives with her parents in Chicago, but there's been no contact."

"So she's hoping to clean up and return to her family and child," Delta guessed.

"Yep. She has strong motivation, which is why I believe she might be a good fit." Jo returned to her office to handle some paperwork and then wandered to Raylene's apartment. Her door was unlocked, but the room was empty.

Her next stop was to inspect the vacant unit, the one Tara would be occupying. The unit was ready for the new resident, so Jo wandered to the mercantile.

She found Raylene inside chatting with her friend, Sherry. The store was almost empty and Jo approached the back counter. "We'll have a full house again tomorrow when Tara, our new resident, arrives."

"Yep, and hopefully things will go smoother this time," Sherry said.

"I've been praying about it." Jo glanced at the clock on the wall. "It's almost closing time. I'll see you inside for dinner. Delta made a big pot of chicken and dumplings."

She exited the mercantile and returned to the house where Delta was pulling a sheet of buttery biscuits from the oven. "Everything in order?" she asked.

"Yes. Tara's unit is ready to go." Jo slumped into the seat and let out a heavy sigh.

"You look like you lost your best friend."

"This whole thing with Raylene. It's like a big, black cloud hanging over my head."

"Mine, too," Delta dropped her oven mitt on the counter and joined Jo. "Not knowing what's going to happen and where she'll be living can't be good for her mentally."

"Or ours either," Jo said. "You should've seen how excited Sherry was the other day when she found out Raylene came back with us."

"They're friends," Delta said. "Friendships are important. This is a tough world."

Jo tilted her head as she studied Delta. "You're right. Friends...real friends are God's gift. I don't know what I would do without you...without Nash and Gary."

"Friends..." Delta drummed her fingers on the table. "You know what? I think I have an idea."

Chapter 22

"An idea?"

"To settle Raylene's future once and for all," Delta said.

"I'm open to any and all suggestions."

"Let's hold a secret vote."

"A secret vote?"

Delta warmed to the idea. "Yeah. At dinner tonight, we'll have the women take turns casting a vote to see if Raylene stays or if she goes."

"There are only four other women. We could easily have a tie," Jo pointed out.

"True. What if we wait until tomorrow night after Tara arrives? Then we'll have five votes."

"It would have to go one way or the other." Jo brightened. "Do you think it would work?"

"I don't see why not."

"Let's do it. I need to chat with Raylene first, to make sure she wants to stay."

"Jo," Delta shook her head. "The woman would be crazy to want to leave here."

"I would hope so, but the decision is hers." Excited at the prospect of a possible solution to Raylene leaving them, Jo hurried back to the mercantile. Sherry was closing up and told Jo that Raylene had gone back to her apartment.

Jo tracked her down there. "Hi, Raylene. I was wondering if you had a few minutes to chat."

Raylene shot Jo a panicked look. "Sure." The woman's steps dragged as she followed Jo to the porch swing. She perched on the edge, her back stiff and her expression somber.

"Don't look so happy," Jo teased as she eased onto the other side.

Duke nudged the screen door open and plodded out to greet them. He sniffed Jo and then made his way to the other end of the swing to greet Raylene. He rested his chin on her leg, eager for attention.

Raylene reached out to pat his head, and then burst into tears.

"Oh, no." Jo slid across the seat, wrapping an arm around the woman. "What's this?"

"I know why I'm here." Raylene's shoulders shook and she began sobbing. "I-I'm sorry."

"Sorry for what?"

"Lord have mercy." Delta, hearing the sobs, ran onto the porch a box of Kleenex in hand. She jerked a handful of tissues from the box and handed them to Raylene. "You're gonna have me bawling in a second."

"I'm sorry for crying." Raylene dabbed at her eyes and then blew her nose. "You decided to send me back to New Beginnings, after all."

Jo dabbed at the tears in her own eyes. "Did I say that?"

"You didn't have to," Raylene hiccupped.

"Scooch over." Delta motioned with her hands and plopped down between them. "Jo and I have an idea."

Raylene sniffled loudly. "What kind of idea?"

"Delta is giving me credit, but she was the one who came up with the idea of having the other women take a vote for you at dinner tomorrow night after Tara, our new resident, arrives. All in favor of you staying here at the farm vote *yes* and all in favor of you leaving vote *no*."

"Seriously?" Raylene brightened.

"Majority rules," Delta said. "Of course, Jo and I can't vote. It would be strictly a vote among your peers."

"I..." Raylene slumped back on the swing. "Then I only have a 50-50 chance of staying."

"Fifty-fifty means the glass is half-full, Raylene. You have a decent shot at staying on." Jo patted her knee. "I'm going to pray about it. I'm sure Delta will pray about it and maybe you should pray about it, too."

"Oh, I do pray," Raylene said. "I thank God every day for saving my life and for bringing me here."

"Then you have nothing to worry about." Jo sounded more confident than she felt, but the talk with Delta and Raylene gave her hope. If it was God's will, then Raylene had already found her new home.

*****

The rest of the day dragged and for the second night in a row, Jo barely slept a wink. Instead, she spent half the night wide-awake and worrying about the arrival of her new resident and Raylene's future.

She finally gave up sleeping in the wee hours of the morning and crept into the kitchen to start a pot of coffee.

Delta found her there a short time later. "What are you doing up?"

"I couldn't sleep."

Delta poured a cup of coffee and plopped down across from Jo. "You're worried about Raylene."

"Yes, and Tara's arrival." Jo sipped her coffee, eyeing her friend over the rim. "Did I make the right decision? Will Tara fit in? Will she get along with the other women?"

"You can second guess yourself all day long, Jo Pepperdine. You do the best you can, pray about it, and let God handle the rest."

"I know," Jo sucked in a breath. "Sometimes it's easier said than done."

"You'll be fine." Delta patted her hand. "We'll be fine."

"Yes, we will." Jo took the last sip of coffee and stood. "I better head upstairs to get ready. Pastor Murphy will be bringing Tara by right after breakfast."

Pastor Murphy arrived promptly at ten. Jo met them on the porch, and then the pastor accompanied Jo as she showed Tara around and introduced her to the other women.

The last stop was Tara's apartment. Pastor Murphy and Jo stood outside while Tara explored her small unit and unpacked her belongings.

"How is Raylene?"

"Relieved she's still here," Jo said.

"I meant to call you yesterday. I had an interesting conversation with the manager of New Beginnings."

"Really?" Jo lifted a brow.

"There was no hostage situation at the group home. It was two doors down. The officer had it wrong. So, with this new information are you sure you want to give up her spot at New Beginnings?"

"Can I give you an answer later this evening?"

The pastor lifted a brow. "Perhaps you've had a change of heart."

"Not on my part. Let's just say, Delta came up with an idea." Jo wagged her finger at him. "Now, don't go getting your hopes up."

"I won't."

Before Jo could reply, Tara joined them, and the two women walked the pastor to his car. After he left, Jo led Tara into the kitchen to introduce her to Delta who promptly put her to work chopping vegetables for the dinner salad.

Tara was a chatterbox, and by the time Jo left she and Delta were talking up a storm.

Jo spent the rest of the day anxiously awaiting the dinner hour and the vote.

Dinner was a lively gathering, with all of the women joining in the conversation and no one more than Tara who, like Delta, possessed a gift for gab. In fact, she turned her prison time into story time making it unnecessary for Jo to ask her to share her story.

Jo's initial takeaway was that others easily influenced Tara. It was something Jo would have to keep an eye on.

Dinner ended, and Jo helped Delta bring in a pot of fresh coffee and crumb cake for dessert.

She made one more trip to the kitchen, returning with a shoebox and some sheets of paper.

"What's this?" Sherry pointed at the box.

"It's time for a vote," Delta motioned to Jo. "I'll let Jo explained."

Jo cleared her throat. "A few days ago, Pastor Murphy, Raylene and I drove to a women's home outside of Kansas City, a new home for Raylene. Without going into too much detail, it didn't work out."

"So she's going to stay," Sherry said.

"Maybe. As you all know." Jo pointed to Tara, "except for Tara, Raylene was incarcerated after a jury convicted her of being an accomplice to murder. I broke one of my own rules by allowing Raylene to stay, but she had nowhere to go, and we were concerned..."

"Jo was concerned I would try to commit suicide a second time," Raylene interrupted.

"Pastor Murphy is working on finding another home for Raylene. After talking with her, Raylene has told me she would like to stay, so Delta came up with an idea." Jo motioned to the women around the table. "You are Raylene's peers. You're her housemates. All of you, except for Tara, have had a chance to get to know her. I'm going to leave it up to you to decide whether Raylene becomes a permanent resident or whether the search continues for her next home."

While Jo explained, Delta walked around the table, handing each of the women...Tara, Sherry, Michelle, Kelli and Leah a slip of paper. "Your vote will be anonymous. While you vote, Raylene and Jo will wait on the porch."

Jo picked up. "A *yes* vote means you want Raylene to stay. A *no* vote means you want Raylene to leave. Any questions?"

The women shook their heads. Jo stood, and she motioned to Raylene. "You're free to discuss it before deciding. Delta will let us know when you're finished."

Jo placed a light hand on Raylene's back, her heart breaking for the poor woman when she felt her body tremble. "It's going to be all right," she whispered.

Raylene nodded her head, not daring to speak.

When they reached the porch, the women sank down on the swing. Jo stared at the dark clouds starting to gather. She nudged the porch floor with her foot, and they began rocking back and forth. "It looks like rain."

"The gardens could use it. I love this place, Jo. Even if I don't get to stay, I want to thank you again for everything you've done for me. You gave me a second chance."

Raylene was silent for a moment. "This isn't a halfway house...it's a home, and a wonderful home at that."

"I...no matter what, it's going to be all right." Jo attempted an encouraging smile, but failed miserably and said the only thing she could think of. "God is in this, Raylene. The decision is his."

"And the other women's."

It was several long moments before Delta appeared in the doorway. "You can come back in now. The women have finished casting their votes."

Chapter 23

Jo followed Raylene inside. All the while, she prayed God's will would be done in the woman's life. Whether it included her staying at *Second Chance* or moving on to another home.

Raylene made her way back to her empty chair and perched on the edge of the seat. She clasped her hands, a tight and solemn expression etched on her face.

Delta cleared her throat. "The votes cast were anonymous and will remain so. As a reminder, a *yes* vote means it's a vote for Raylene to stay. A *no* is a vote for her to leave."

She waited for Jo to resume her place at the head of the table before removing the lid on the shoebox and unfolding the first sheet of paper. "Vote one of five...yes."

Delta plucked out a second slip of paper. "Another yes."

"Vote number three...no."

Raylene's shoulders slumped, and she lowered her head.

"We have two more left," Delta said. "It could go either way."

She unfolded the fourth small slip of paper and stared at it for what seemed like an eternity.

"C'mon, Delta. You're torturing us," Jo groaned.

"Another yes." Delta released her grip on the slip of paper and it fluttered to the floor. "I don't need to read the last vote. Three 'yes' votes mean Raylene is welcome to stay."

Raylene began shaking uncontrollably, tears streaming down her cheeks.

Sherry sprang from her chair and ran to her friend's side, wrapping both arms around her. "Happy tears. You get to stay!"

"I want to stay more than anything," Raylene whispered.

Jo waited until the others finished hugging Raylene before kneeling next to her chair. "This truly is your second chance. You must still abide by all of the house rules, and I know that you will. I'm thrilled with the decision and can't wait to see what your future holds."

Jo gave her arm a gentle squeeze and stood. "What *all* of your futures hold. Now, I'm going to call Pastor Murphy to let him know he can stop searching for a place. You're staying right here with us."

By the time Jo returned to the dining room, the women had left, leaving only Delta in the kitchen, and Raylene hovering in the doorway.

"I-I just wanted to let you know how much this means to me," Raylene's voice cracked. "I want to start going to church with you on Sunday if that's all right."

Jo's heart skipped a beat. It was the first time Raylene had showed an interest in attending church.

Jo never pushed the residents, although she encouraged each of them to attend the Sunday morning service at least once. "That would be wonderful," Jo said.

Raylene gave Jo a shy smile and turned to go.

Without warning, she turned back, hurtling herself at Jo and knocking her off balance. "Thank you. Thank you so much. I don't know how I'm ever going to be able to repay you."

"You're welcome, Raylene. One day I will watch you leave *Second Chance* with your head held high, ready to take on the world." Jo briefly closed her eyes, thanking God for his miracles as she returned the warm embrace before taking a step back. "Welcome home."

The end.

If you enjoyed reading "Divine Secrets," please take a moment to leave a review. It would mean so much to me. Thank you! Hope Callaghan

The series continues... Book 3 in the Divine Cozy Mystery Series coming soon!

Meet the Author

Hope loves to connect with her readers! Connect with her today!

Never miss another book deal! Text the word Books to 33222

Visit **hopecallaghan.com/newsletter** for special offers, free books, and new releases!

Follow On Facebook:
www.facebook.com/authorhopecallaghan/

Follow On Amazon:
www.amazon.com/HopeCallaghan/e/B00OJ5X702

Follow On Pinterest:
www.pinterest.com/cozymysteriesauthor/

Hope Callaghan is an American author who loves to write Christian books, especially Christian Mystery and Cozy Mystery books. She has written more than 50 mystery books (and counting) in six series.

In March 2017, Hope won a Mom's Choice Award for her book, "Key to Savannah," Book 1 in the Made in Savannah Cozy Mystery Series.

Born and raised in a small town in West Michigan, she now lives in Florida with her husband.

She is the proud mother of one daughter and a stepdaughter and stepson. When she's not doing the thing she loves best - writing books - she enjoys cooking, traveling and reading books.

Delta's Divine BBQ Chicken Slider Recipe

Ingredients:

1 – 14 oz. container chicken broth

3 pounds boneless, skinless chicken breasts

Delta's Kansas City BBQ Sauce (recipe below)

Directions:

-Pour container of chicken broth into slow cooker.

-Add boneless, skinless chicken breasts.

-Cook chicken breasts on high for four hours.

-Remove chicken from crockpot. Let cool and then shred with a fork.

-Discard broth (or save for soup broth!)

-Return meat to crockpot.

-Add Delta's Kansas City BBQ sauce (recipe below.)

-Stir thoroughly. Cook on low for 30 minutes.

-Serve on small roll.

Delta's BBQ Sauce Recipe

Ingredients:

½ yellow onion, minced

4 cloves garlic, minced

1 tsp. of vanilla extract

½ tsp. ground black pepper

½ tablespoon salt

2 cups ketchup

¼ cup tomato paste

1/3 cup apple cider vinegar

2 tablespoons liquid smoke flavoring (we used Figaro brand)

¼ cup Worcestershire sauce

½ cup packed brown sugar

1/3 tsp. hot pepper sauce*

½ tsp. lemon juice

Directions:

-In large skillet or pot, combine the onion, garlic

and vanilla.

-Sauté onion and garlic in a small amount of butter, stir in the vanilla.

-Add remaining ingredients and bring to a boil.

-Reduce heat to medium-low. Simmer for 20 minutes.

Made in United States
North Haven, CT
14 February 2024

48759995R00190